At last—— appened then?"

In the now classic "Planet of the Apes," 20th-century man discovered that a strange world of the future was his own Earth. In this sequel, which begins exactly where the first story ended, man explores deeper into the incredible wasteland that he himself created. Startling contrasts between familiar sights—the Statue of Liberty, St. Patrick's Cathedral, a subway station, New York City—and the rubble of centuries, which has covered the earth, give way to the shocking discovery of a mutated race of humans who worship the instrument which created their world—the Doomsday Bomb.

Science fiction, monster picture, western-type adventure, love story, war intrigue—**BENEATH THE PLANET OF THE APES** is the best of all of these in one spectacular story.

20th CENTURY-FOX
presents

AN ARTHUR P. JACOBS PRODUCTION

BENEATH THE PLANET OF THE APES

Starring

JAMES FRANCISCUS
KIM HUNTER
MAURICE EVANS
LINDA HARRISON

Co-starring
PAUL RICHARDS
VICTOR BUONO
JAMES GREGORY
JEFF COREY
NATALIE TRUNDY
THOMAS GOMEZ

and
CHARLTON HESTON
as
Taylor

Produced by
APJAC PRODUCTIONS

Associate Producer
MORT ABRAHAMS

Directed by
TED POST

Screenplay by
PAUL DEHN

Story by
PAUL DEHN and
MORT ABRAHAMS

Based upon Characters Created by
PIERRE BOULLE

Music by
LEONARD ROSENMAN

PANAVISION ®
Color by De Luxe

BENEATH THE PLANET OF THE APES

By Michael Avallone

Screenplay by Paul Dehn
Story by Paul Dehn and Mort Abrahams
Based upon Characters Created by Pierre Boulle

BANTAM BOOKS
TORONTO · LONDON
NEW YORK
A NATIONAL GENERAL COMPANY

BENEATH THE PLANET OF THE APES
A Bantam Book / published July 1970

Published simultaneously in the United States and Canada

Bantam Books are published by Bantam Books, Inc., a National
General company. Its trade-mark, consisting of the words "Bantam
Books" and the portrayal of a bantam, is registered in the United
States Patent Office and in other countries. Marca Registrada.
Bantam Books, Inc., 666 Fifth Avenue, New York, N.Y. 10019.

PRINTED IN THE UNITED STATES OF AMERICA

For Pierre Boulle
for his two very important
contributions to the arts of
Literature and Film—
The Bridge Over The River Kwai
and *Planet Of The Apes.*

Contents

1.	GENESIS	1
2.	TAYLOR	3
3.	BRENT	15
4.	URSUS	26
5.	ZIRA AND CORNELIUS	36
6.	NOVA	46
7.	BRENT AND NOVA	57
8.	SPECTERS	67
9.	MENDEZ	76
10.	MASKS	88
11.	*"TAY-LOR!"*	100
12.	DR. ZAIUS	110
13.	APE AND MAN	119
14.	BOMB	129
15.	ARMAGEDDON	133

BENEATH THE
PLANET
OF THE APES

1 GENESIS

Wasteland.

Total, glaring, absolute.

Stark, terrible.

Nothing growing.

Nothing moving.

Ageless, perpetual silence. Eternal solitude. Only the piercing whine of the dry nameless wind blowing in from a distantly heard sea.

Desolation. A universe of nakedness and nil.

Utter, supreme. Everlasting.

Nothing of Life. Only the unrelenting deathly stillness. The infinity of zero, emptiness, nothingness.

This is the planet where Man has lost his supreme position in the scheme of things. Listen to the Wind.

If it could speak, it would tell you of Taylor. The man, the scientist, the space-explorer. The scorching, chilling breath of the wind's passage would carry the terrible tale to the walls of Infinity, down the endless corridors of that vast timelessness which seems to be the core of the land itself . . .

Listen, the Wind . . .

"This is the truth eternal: whatever thinks, can speak. And whatever speaks can murder.

"But what is there to murder in this dead place?"

There is no answer for the Wind.

"When the astronaut, Taylor, came first among us from a voyage in outermost space, he perceived that his ship had passed through a fold in the Fourth Dimension, which is Time. And Taylor knew that he was older than when his journey had begun . . . by two thousand years and ten."

The Wind whines higher and louder, scoring eerily over a dead landscape. Weird lambent lights suffuse the terrain. There is a vast unearthly brilliance invested in a panorama of Nothingness.

"But in the first days he did not know the name of the planet on which he had set foot—where Apes, risen to great estate, had acquired the power of tongues, while Man, fallen from his zenith to become a beast of the earth, had lost the means of speech, and was dumb . . ."

The dead sands remained unmoving, the wind prowled over the monolithic expanse of desert-like desolation. And isolation. The unknown lights bathed the wasteland with a dull, inflexible glow.

"Now Taylor hated war. And since Man had made war upon himself—murdered himself—over and over again, ever since the first town was built and burned and bloodied—Taylor believed that the race of Man was hopeless."

A Dead Sea. Dead like the Dead Land.

The wind stole quietly over the still, stagnant, murky waters.

"Yet the great Apes were hardly better. They put Taylor in a cage as they had once been caged. When he and his woman escaped from the City of the Apes into the wilderness called the Forbidden Zone . . . he found a desert land of rock and stone. Barren, unfruitful, devoid of life and eternally laid waste by Man's vilest war in Man's history. And in this wilderness, Taylor set eyes upon the Statue . . ."

A statue with spikes.

A stone lady, gazing out over the limitless endless acres of sand. Oblivious to the mean waves lapping at her copper-lined bosom. A Colossus, with upstretched arm, bearing aloft a torch that had lost all its meaning. All its truth. All its light.

A long-dead lady of stone eyes, stone ears and stone senses——whose only companion for an eon had been——

—the Wind.

"*. . . and Taylor knew he was back on Earth . . . an Earth defiled and destroyed by the hand of Man. Set this down: whatever speaks, can murder.*"

And Taylor, sliding down from the back of his horse, with the savage woman Nova also dismounting, staggered toward the gigantic spikes upthrusting from the cruel sand and blurted his cry of agony to the unheeding skies all around them: "*Goddamn you all to hell!*"

Falling to his torn knees, he buried his head in his hands. Sobs racked his tall, magnificent figure. Nova watched and listened in dumb incomprehension. The dead landscape remained mute.

The Statue of Liberty could not hear Taylor weeping.

Stone has no heart.

Or soul.

It does not even hear the wind.

2   TAYLOR

Taylor and the girl, Nova, departed wearily from the staggering spectacle before them. Behind them, the half-buried statue of Miss Liberty beckoned mutely from her sandy grave. The dead waters lapped pitifully at her stone shoulders and obsidian face.

Taylor's mind reeled.

He was rendered incapable of any thought but that of the greatest wonder.

The scientist in him was mocked.

The space-explorer in him was confounded.

The man in him was brutally stunned.

The nameless planet, ruled by a hierarchy of intelligent apes was *This Planet Earth!* Or rather, more bizarrely, more fittingly, what was left of it.

His own imagination, his own instincts and senses, boggled before the import of what he had seen. What he now knew for an unalterable fact. The world as he had known it, when he had left Earth for outer space with his three fellow scientists, was now a madhouse. A mathematical equation of unequivocal madness and nonsense.

Even as he wandered futilely across the arid desert stretches of this monumental Nowhere, with Nova limply and stickily plastered to his back astride the poor, tired horse, he tried to sort out the memories and experiences of the most recent past.

How long ago had it been that he and the three others, one of them a woman, had lost their way in limitless space and come down on this alien soil in their ailing spacecraft? Time and torture at the hands of the militant apes had robbed Taylor of his ability to think. Now he could not even remember the names of his space comrades. All he could recall was the terrible incident of landing. The woman had been dead, on first contact with the terrain. It was not the physical hardship of a crash landing but the inherent qualities of the flight itself. All four astronauts, through some intricate process aboard the spacecraft, had aged eighteen months in a time lapse of 2000 years from Earth. Being female, the woman had not survived the flight. Taylor and the two men had swum for shore, reaching a wasteland of Arizona-like proportions. All brown dry earth and long shelves of rock stretching as far as the eye could see. It was then that the men from Earth reached some form of vegetation in their aimless wanderings and encountered the horde of filthy, unkempt, savage, barbaric humans who had lost the power of speech—if they had ever had it. Nova had been one of them. A long-haired, wild-eyed beauty who could do no more than look at you with her eyes to convey her meaning. Someone you had to teach how to smile!

Then, sweeping down through the bushes and the trees, had come the cavalry of apes. Leather-jacketed, truncheon-wielding, rifle-shooting gorillas. The barbaric whites had tried to run; Taylor and his two comrades among them. Terrified, speechless with horror. With whips, nets and hooks, the militia of gorillas had rounded them all up, killing those who dared to fight back. One of Taylor's crew died in the attack. But the worst part of the whole bloody nightmare was what followed.

Taylor found himself led to a complex. An area of stone warrens, of houses and cages, where the ape was the ruler of all that was left of the civilization on this planet. It was a simian state, ruled by a kingdom of gorillas, with chimpanzees and orangutans serving as medical men. Of the remaining two astronauts, one was lobotomized and converted into an unthinking vegetable. For Taylor, the simian rulers decreed emasculation and a brainwashing which would eradicate his memory. But with the help of chimpanzee scientists, who felt the ape autocracy was far from a benevolent one, Taylor had made his escape. With Nova. A doglike, mute love had sprung up between them because the girl could not speak. Might never speak though Taylor had tried to teach her.

And now that he had found his way into the Forbidden Zone, leaving his tormentors God knew how far behind, Taylor could still remember the unbelievable aura and reality of the Ape Kingdom. The signs all over the place: THE ALMIGHTY CREATED THE APE IN HIS OWN IMAGE——ONLY HUMANS KILL FOR SPORT, LUST OR GREED . . . HUMAN SEE, HUMAN DO . . . and all those incredible statues and artifacts of ape culture: the hear-no-evil-see-no-evil-speak-no-evil symbol; the mother gorilla holding a baby ape in her arms like Michelangelo's *Pieta*, the whole abominable concept of Ape as Human Being!

Yes, Taylor remembered that much.

The shock might never wear off.

With humans in cages, people being whipped and driven, the race of mankind lorded and ruled by a panel of intellectual apes who had revised the entire scheme of the order of heredity and nature. It was something that would haunt whatever was left of his own life . . .

Ape had evolved from Man.

Detecting menace and extinction from the twin conditions of human ignorance and bestiality, the society of apes had presumed that their own well-being depended upon the mastery and domination of the inferior being known as Man. It was a thoroughgoing example of genocide in action, as Taylor had actually seen it.

Man as slave labor, Man as expendable creature, Man as Nothing.

The world had come to a fitting irony after another 2000 years of Knowledge, Culture and Freedom. It had descended back to the apes, climbed back into the same tree from which it had escaped.

And all it had obviously needed to upset the applecart had been one madman's thermonuclear bomb.

Some nation's plunge into the Final Solution. Whose? America? France? Red China? Russia? Germany? England? Israel . . . ?

It didn't matter, now.

It was Man's epitaph, no matter how you looked at it.

Whether as man, scientist or space-explorer.

The wheel had come full cycle.

There was nothing left——but death.

Their aimless, sluggish trek across the vast waste-land had been an amalgam of scorching heat, discomfort and mind-pounding weariness. Taylor could hardly feel the bones in his body. Bearded, bronzed, clothed in fragments of leather garment, he felt like some archaic Adam lost in a new world. Nova, her lithe body hugging him, was as silent as ever. The poor mare accommodating them both had almost lost the power to move.

The sun beat down from a blue sky hazed with white clouds. Taylor's eyeballs ached. The sweat ran down his strong-planed face and gauntly formidable shoulders.

They saw the oasis at the same time. The girl almost frantically pummeled his back. Taylor nodded. It was there, all right. No mirage, no trickery. The country was as arid as ever but he could clearly see trees, a pool of oddly clear water. The dark scowl which had been fixed like a graven image on Taylor's face, lifted.

Slowly he led the horse to the water's edge, staring down. Yes, it was real. He could see their reflections in the low pool. It was no more than a waterhole, flanked by low, gnarled trees which perhaps had never known foliage.

"Water," Taylor murmured. "But the trees are dead."

He helped Nova dismount, never unaware completely of the fine animal body, the nubile beauty of her. Nova's eyes were like two eternal question marks. As if existence itself were something for which she could never find the answer.

Taylor leaned over the water, testing it tentatively. It seemed all right. It wasn't brackish or foreign-tasting. He gestured to Nova and pulled the horse over. All three drank. Lustily, busily, as though it were the most important single act in the world.

Sated, Taylor flopped back on the sand, staring up at the remorselessly hot sky. Nova came over to him, lying down dutifully, and he locked an arm around her, still staring up.

His blue eyes slitted sardonically. It might be a sky anywhere in a normal universe. A mantle over New York on a summer day. Or Vermont or Kansas. Or Arizona . . . it was over New York, all right. A Manhattan or a Brooklyn or a Bronx buried under hundreds of feet of thermonuclear sand. What a travesty!

"Where in hell do we go from here?" he growled up at the sky. There was no answer. He twisted to look at Nova. "Or do we just stop off and found a human colony? And the kids would learn to talk——better sense than the apes."

Suddenly he placed a bronzed forefinger on Nova's lips. Those full, uncosmetized labias that made of her face an appealing miracle.

"Try to say the name I gave you," he commanded softly. "*No-va.*"

She remained mystified and mute, as always. He pointed at her, conscious of the surge of her splendid body against its pitiful fragments of costume. Then he pointed again, each time repeating her name as if it were a litany.

"*No-va . . . No-va . . . No-va . . .*"

Still she remained mute, her eyes puzzled.

Then, and to his intense pleasure, she pointed her own finger at him, peering closely into his eyes.

"*Taylor*," Taylor said, understanding what she was after.

She pointed once more.

"*Taylor*," he echoed his own name.

She squinted in the sun. "*Taylor*," he said again, watching her mouth. Her lips were struggling with a sound but nothing came forth. A dumb and mute Eve. Beautiful but incommunicado.

From among the rags of his body, Taylor produced his identity tag. The metallic ID from another world, another time. He looped it around his own neck and pointed to it. The disc gleamed in the sunlight. Nova followed his every move, like a child trying to learn.

"*Tay-lor—*" he said, very slowly and carefully.

Her lips barely moved in a brave attempt at mimicry. But no sound issued. Taylor sighed. Nova frowned, still trying. He reached across and kissed her tenderly on the lips, as he struggled to his feet. It would take more time than they had now . . .

"Let's find a home," Taylor said.

Home.

It was not to be found in the limitless mass of wasteland. They plodded on, the horse dutifully carrying their combined weight. The sun beat down, a remote circle of fire far above in the leaden skies. Taylor guided the horse up a long slope that closed off any view of the horizon and what might lay before them. Nova clung to him like a frightened child.

Finally, they had cleared the crest of the slope.

Taylor halted in stupefaction, checking the horse with a violent tug.

It was a view from Hell.

A huge burial mound of scattered rock and rubble, stretching as far as the eye could see. Like some endless cemetery in which, like small and large tombstones, jutted the recognizable artifacts of a civilization long since destroyed and—*ended*. The ravaged and identifiable tops of Manhattan's major skyscrapers shone dully in the glare. The pointed spire of the Chrysler Building, the powerful snub of the Empire State, the symmetrical squared roof of the RCA Building and the glittering, glasslike——

Taylor blinked, closed his eyes and opened them again.

The vision did not dissolve or shimmer or go away.

Bitterly, his heart dying within him, he knew he was staring at the remnants of a long-since-buried New York.

Nova murmured uneasily behind him. An animal sound.

A low, hissing wind stole over the devastated landscape.

"Well—" Taylor said softly, more to himself than to the girl. "Home sweet home! Just look at this graveyard, Nova. It's the grand climax of fifty thousand years of human culture—yes. I wonder who lives here now. Besides radioactive worms."

No answer came.

Like all dead things, ruined New York was inscrutable.

"Let's go see," Taylor said to the girl and urged their mount down the slope toward the big graveyard before them. There was still nothing but those masses of scrub and tombstones. Nova suddenly plucked urgently at Taylor's arm. She beckoned wildly.

Taylor looked, gaping.

Unbelievably, a tremendous change had swept over the panorama below. A huge, inexplicable wall of fire had sprung up directly in their path. It seemed to have started in the shrubbery, cutting amazingly across the bare rock and sand, building into a raging inferno of heat and brightness. The horse reared on its hind legs, neighing in terror. The high barrier of flame, crackling and sending out great waves of scorching heat, completely concealed buried New York from view. It had seemed to vanish in the twinkling of an eye.

"What—what the hell's *feeding* it?" Taylor bellowed hoarsely. "There's nothing to burn."

The horse had U-turned violently, almost flinging the two of them off. Taylor cursed and hung on. The crackling flames licked ever nearer, closing in on them. Now the horse took to the gallop, racing away from the unknown, plunging down the slope again, leaving New York and the incredible wall of fire hidden below the horizon.

"We'll reach it another way," Taylor said grimly, urging the horse forward in a flanking movement. He meant to circle the city and approach from another direction. From the inland side, far removed from the mysterious blaze and its source.

They passed the oasis once more, pushed on over the open, trackless dry wastes until the horse's hooves touched a flattened plain which afforded easier going. The cloudless blue sky showed the empty horizon beyond the plain. Taylor made for it, conscious of a nagging confusion in his brain and Nova's mutelike trust in him.

"Okay, here we go again."

He had to talk, had to say something. Whether the girl understood him or not. Hearing his own voice was a measure of reality in a universe gone mad.

He turned the horse to make a second approach.

But the unrealities had mounted.

Scarcely had they started when a colossal clap of thunder shook the heavens and instantly, magically, black clouds roiled, the skies darkened overhead, and within seconds the world turned black. From below the far horizon, rods of forked lightning struck. The horse reared in bewilderment and terror. Like glitter-

ing stakes in an electrified fence, each lightning rod
struck down to the earth. What was worse, they
seemed to advance toward Taylor, the girl and the
horse. Advance relentlessly to the accompaniment of
vicious thunderclaps. And then rain, fiercely falling,
hissing rain, sluiced down in blinding sheets. The sky,
so recently blue, had opened up into a sea of dark fury.
The horse kept on rearing, whinnying, bellowing its
terror. Taylor fought the beast, keeping it from bolt-
ing altogether in the face of nature's onslaught.

"Nature seems bent—" Taylor panted, "on wiping
out our mistake. Hold it!" He struck at the horse,
holding its head while Nova huddled behind him. Their
drenched bodies fused in limp, liquid union. At a
gallop, they retreated from the sonic, sodden storm.
The horse kept on racing until the thunder and the
rain diminished. Until they had found a blue sky again
and the miracle of a nature gone beserk was behind
them. Taylor reined the flagging horse to a standstill.
Then he turned it around again for still a third approach to the New York that lay buried in the distance.
He was determined—it was mad of him, he suspected
—to go back to that dead land. He couldn't have said
why it was important to him.

But the world was truly mad.

The elements had run amuck.

Nature was still awry.

Rising directly in his path—his, the girl's and their
horse—was a wall of ice. A thick, glassy, solid, un-
melting barrier of ice. A paradox of eye and mind,
giving the lie to the bright ball of sun blazing down
from the blue sky above.

Taylor's mind stopped.

He was frightened now, really frightened. The awesome mass of crystal towering down dwarfed all his
logic, all his strength.

"That wasn't here," he murmured. "A minute ago,

that wasn't here!" He turned to Nova; the girl was cowering behind him, hiding her eyes from the terrible apparition. "And it isn't just me who's seeing things," Taylor breathed scratchily. He steadied the horse's restive head. "Can two people have the same nightmare?"

Shocked, he led the horse away from the precipice of ice. The girl hugged him, her nails digging into his weary body. Taylor shook himself dumbly. Before he could make another move, a tremendous, seismic crescendo of sound rumbled behind him. The girl blurted a scream. Taylor caught himself in time. A gigantic fissure, as palpable as death and fear itself, had yawned in the earth and Taylor desperately managed to career the horse so that it avoided the mammoth canyon of nothingness that had suddenly loomed before its hooves. Thank God the poor beast was sufficiently exhausted for him to control it. If it had bolted suddenly . . .

Taylor turned to Nova. Urgency made him mime the words he spoke to her now. It was imperative that she understand him.

"Nova! If *you*—" he pointed to her, "lose—*me*—" he pointed to himself, "go to Ape City." She recoiled in horror at the words. He shook his head. "Not to the gorillas. Go to the chimpanzee quarter. There's no other way." He fought against the incomprehension in her terrified eyes. "Find Zira. *Zi-ra* . . ."

She nodded now, less fearfully, recognizing the name of the sympathetic female chimpanzee doctor who had helped them escape to the Forbidden Zone. But she clung to his hand, not letting go until she knew he wished it. Taylor dismounted from the horse, purposefully unslinging the rifle from the bolster on the saddle. There was now a ten-yard ledge between the crevice and the precipice of ice. Taylor shook himself once again, feeling his brains boiling over.

"Impossible! But it's there—I'm not dreaming. Or else I—or maybe the whole universe—has gone mad!"

He advanced furiously on the ice face.

Nova, on the horse, watched him, fright fixing her face.

Taylor used the butt of the rifle, attempting to chop out a foothold. The gun cut a swath through the air. Taylor followed through hard. Yet the phenomena, the amazements, the unrealities, were a long way from done.

The rifle struck. With a flick of sound.

And passed *clean through* the wall of ice, vanishing.

Taylor, unbalanced by the unexpected lack of resistance, followed the vicious swath of the rifle.

And also vanished.

It was as if he had stepped through a bead curtain.

There was nothing on the ice face of the precipice to indicate where he had been. Or had gone.

And then the wall of ice was gone too.

It was nowhere to be seen.

There wasn't anything anywhere for miles around but the flat, ordinary, cruel wasteland. The landscape was completely deserted.

The girl Nova screamed.

And kept on screaming.

Until her screams were lost in the vast wilderness of silence.

Until there was Nothing.

3   BRENT

He clambered through the open escape hatch, carrying the vital medical equipment and oxygen apparatus. The crumpled steel sides of the small reconnaissance spacecraft had never seemed so vulnerable to him. Now, set down in a crash landing on some unknown, perhaps alien planet, it was twice as toylike and futile. Being lost in space was one thing, but this was the penultimate in Nowhere. Never had he seen so much limitless desert waste, so much unending distance between things. He felt like a small boy wandering amidst the vast trackless expanses of Time itself. There was no telling where Life began—or ended.

The skipper was still lying where he had left him. Head propped on a mound of sand, his rugged body spent and looking for all the world like a battered rag doll. The impact of the crash had banged the skipper up plenty. There was no immediate telling the extent of the personal damage.

As he bent over the skipper, the equipment clattered metallically. The skipper stirred, eyes open, face haggard in the fierce blaze of an unseen sun.

"Who's that?" The question was a feeble attempt at authority.

"Me again, Skipper."

He passed his hand twice over his superior's eyes. He saw that they did not flicker at all.

"Brent?"

"Sir?"

Skipper was breathing with great difficulty now. Brent busied himself quickly. First he gave Skipper a pill, then an efficient injection by hypodermic in the left arm, and then settled down to a rhythmic, powerful chest massage with his bare hands. Skipper almost smiled at that but the look in the dulled brown eyes was remote, distant, as though fixed on some faraway place that only he could see. The emblem swatches of the United States flag sewn into the left sleeve of the tunics both men wore, shone like blood in the tropical blaze of daylight. Brent resisted the mental image.

"Did you contact Earth?" Skipper rasped, his voice getting weaker with each breath he drew.

"Tried to, sir. Not a crackle."

"Isn't the set operational?"

Brent frowned. "I don't know, sir. I ran a crosscheck of the Operations Manual. As suggested, I took an Earth-Time reading just before re-entry."

"Well?"

"Three—nine—five—five." Brent spaced the numbers very very slowly, as if he still couldn't believe them himself.

"Hours?" Skipper stirred again, almost trying to rise. Brent steadied him with a firm restraining hand. "There are only twenty-four . . ."

"Not hours," Brent said. "*Years.*"

Skipper breathed hoarsely. The unseeing eyes seemed to freeze.

"Three thousand—nine hundred—and fifty-five?"

"A.D." Brent agreed, drily.

"Almighty God."

In the brief silence, both men might have been listening to the hissing, scorching wind sweeping over the baking landscape.

"We were following Taylor's trajectory," Brent continued, trying to hang onto his calm. "So whatever happened to us, must have happened to Taylor—" he continued to massage his superior's chest.

"What about us? Where are we?"

Skipper sounded like a desperate blind man, trying to see what he never might again.

"In my opinion, sir, we've come through a Hasslein Curve, a bend in Time."

Skipper groaned feebly, falling back in greater pain than before. The damning facts had only augmented his poor condition. Brent tried to rally him, knowing how hopeless that was on the face of it. His superior, by all the signs, was a dying man.

"Look," Brent spoke rapidly. "I don't know what planet we're on. I know it's fantastic but the fact is, we're both of us here, wherever that is. Breathing. Conscious. There's oxygen on this planet—and water. You'll be okay, Skipper. We'll run a navigational estimate . . ."

The unseeing man at his side stared mightily up into the alien sky. His face was bleached, almost lifeless.

"God, if I could only see the sun!"

"You can feel it on your hand, Skipper," Brent said very quietly. But his brain wasn't quiet at all. It was rioting.

"Yes—but which sun?"

"I don't know. Our computer is shot. We're lucky to be alive."

"Lucky—?" Skipper echoed with sudden fury and strength. "No! If it's A.D. 3955——oh, God! My wife ——" His breathing was obviously becoming more difficult. "My two daughters. Dead. Their sons. Daughters. Dead. Everyone I ever knew. Everyone!"

"Yes, sir," Brent agreed, more quiet than ever. "But I'm trying not to believe it." He was too, with every fibre and atom of his being and reasoning power. "It's quiet here, sir. God, it's quiet."

It was. There was no sound, no movement, save for the almost furtive whisper of that phantom wind hurrying over the limitless expanses of sandy soil. This unknown planet was a wasteland.

Skipper suddenly pressed both deadening hands against his own chest and choked violently, desperately.

"Oxygen—" he gasped. "More . . ."

Brent leaped to obey, his heart hammering, his pulses pounding. Not even all of the intense, highly technological education instilled in him by the Space Program had ever prepared him for this. Sudden Death is forever a blow, a shock to the nervous system, no matter where, when or how it strikes.

Within the next torrid hour, he was burying Skipper. Shoveling sand over a rough grave just beyond the dune where the spacecraft had crashed to earth. A melancholy assignment, endured with aching muscles and ragged nerve ends, with tears poised on the lids of each eye. Brent was a young, athletic, handsome astronaut; clear-eyed, level-headed, with the look of eagles in his eyes. But Skipper's dying reduced him to a terribly lonely and frightened young scientist.

He felt like a small boy lost in a maze.

It was only when he had patted the last shovel of loose sand over Skipper's grave that the man in him returned. The one who had wanted to explore outer space and learn the secrets of the skies.

For it was then that he heard the first sound of life on this planet since the spacecraft had come down; the initial indication that other forms of animal life existed on this unknown, blazing chunk of *terra firma* beyond the stars.

He heard the clopping sounds of the horse's hooves long before he saw the beast and the savage-looking female riding it.

Nova, forlorn and aimlessly wandering since the strange disappearance of Taylor, had blundered across the path of the wrecked reconnaissance spacecraft. Another lost child.

Brent watched her from the concealment of the sand dune overshadowing Skipper's grave. He didn't make a move until it looked as if Nova would continue on her way. The horse was balky, frightened.

Then he sprang erect, looming before her path, waving his arms, calling out "Hi!" like a maniac, blocking the way.

Nova stared down at him, her gaze torn between him and the shining wreckage of the spacecraft. Brent came closer, cautiously, quietly now, not wanting to frighten her off.

"Who are you?"

Nova did not answer.

"Can you understand me?"

Nova continued to stare, eyes uncomprehending. Brent came still closer. As bewildered as he was, he decided he had never seen a more beautiful, primeval-looking female in all his life. She might have stepped out of one of those old Tarzan movies of the twentieth century.

"Don't be frightened," he said easily, smiling to make it more palatable. "Just tell me where I am."

Still she did not answer.

"My name is Brent." He reached out to touch the horse's nose in a gesture of friendliness. "Brent——!" With the same fervor which had characterized Taylor's attempts, Brent mimed his own name, pointing to himself with grand gestures. Nova gazed down at him, unblinking. It was impossible to tell what she was thinking, what her attitude might be. Brent felt defeat rise in his chest but he shook it off.

"I'm not going to hurt you—I just want to know where I am. Where are you from? Where are your people? How do I get to them? Which way? Can you talk?" He paused, watching her closely. He had his answer in her mute, unspoken demeanor. "You can't talk."

Bitterly, he shook the rage out of his brain. The defeat.

Then his eye caught sight of the identification tag looped about her dusky throat where its bright disc caught the rays of the fierce sunlight.

"You have a name—?" She didn't flinch as he reached up to turn the tag toward his own eyes so that he could read it. In that single instant, Brent felt all the miracle of rebirth. And a hope for Tomorrow. The name TAYLOR, clearly imprinted on the disc, set off rockets in his heart, soul and mind. "TAYLOR! Is he alive? Is he hurt?"

Now, for the very first time, Nova came to life. Her eyes lit up, showing emotional response. She nodded excitedly. Once, twice, three times. Her whole body seemed to take on new vitality. The horse shifted its weight with her movements. Brent, now more desperate than ever to make himself understood, literally seized on all the play-acting ability at his command. He was using sign language, gestures, vocal emphasis to get through to this strange young woman, who had wandered from nowhere to find him.

"Look . . . is there anyone . . . any other . . . someone who can talk . . . ?"

Nova smiled at that, dismounting from the horse.

Brent took heart.

"*You*—" he pointed to her, "take *me*—to *Taylor*."

Her smile widened. A dazzling, marvelous smile that rivaled the sun overhead. She relooped the ID tag about her throat. Without asking her permission, Brent quickly mounted the horse directly behind her back. She started at that, staring at him, uttering a tiny cry of dismay. Brent grinned, urged the horse forward and motioned her to mount behind him. With a glad cry, she did so, huddling against his shoulders. Brent looked at her, just once more.

Their eyes met. Held.

"Taylor," he said. "*Now*."

The dazzling smile once more washed over him.

"Where?" he asked.

She held onto him, even more closely than before. He could see that her gaze was focused intently toward the right. Whatever direction of the compass that might be.

"All right," he said. "We'll just ride on—till we run out of gas."

With that, he broke the horse into a slow trot over the scorched, baked dunes. Leaving the spacecraft, Skipper's grave, and the greatest mystery of his life behind him.

Temporarily, at least.

There was only one thing left in the universe, A.D. 3955 or not.

Find Taylor.

The search became a trek. A wearying, parching, searing exodus across a land which might have sprung whole from the pages of the Old Testament. Never had Brent known so much desert, so much sun, so much dry, sandy, barren nothingness. There was nothing to be seen of a horizon, for the mantle of blazing heat and cloudless skies seemed to blend in waves of infernal, dancing heat which made vision valueless and pointless beyond more than five hundred yards. It was as if this strange planet lay like a skeleton bleaching beneath the ferocity of a never-extinguished sunlight. Night seemed an impossibility. It was difficult to assess anything. Neither place, Time nor direction. Brent could only let the horse plod along in a forward direction and hope for the best. The girl clinging to his dampened body was like some lovely homunculus growing out of his very back. Brent could barely see straight. His eyeballs ached, he had difficulty keeping his lids open. Great weights pressed down on his eyelids. And all about him, and the girl, beat down a heat so furnace-like and unrelenting that he felt as if the blood within his flesh was boiling. Time crawled, droned on. Not even the random furtive breeze which intermittently made its presence known by hissing across this blasted panorama of a Death Valley could relieve the depressing sensation of parboiled desolation and extinct living matter. Nothing could live in this inferno. Nothing. Brent was forcibly reminded of the many sites of atomic bomb testings on Earth where he had experienced this selfsame feeling of utter loss and obliteration. This vast, barren wasteland was exactly like that. He had not seen so much as an ant crawling across the ground. Not even the indestructible ant could have survived in this mass of deadness.

Not even Taylor . . .

He pushed the dismal conclusion from what was left of his thinking mind and pushed the poor horse on. Behind him, Nova made small, almost mewing sounds from time to time. Dimly, he wondered who she was, who she might be and where in God's name she had come from. Surely she hadn't grown to such lush womanhood, no matter how savagely formed, in a desert horrorland like this! It was inconceivable. Even a rudimentary knowledge of biology and ethnics told him that. Ecologically, the girl could never have bloomed in a Hades like this desert. Which had to mean that she came from somewhere else. Somewhere —where there was a normal sun, fresh air and green grass and . . .

Brent's head toyed with mirages. With vistas of cool, rippling water and waving palm trees and fresh offshore winds. He caught hold of himself and steadied the horse on a plodding path over the wretched, fruit-less terrain. Before them, many more endless stretches of rock and dune glistened cruelly in the sunlight.

The mirage moved from the boundaries of his mind and set itself down before him. Twinkling. Iridescent, like a pearl.

He blinked in the scorching sunlight.

His tongue licked greedily at his parched lips.

His pulses quickened.

He saw the greenness, the lushness, the beckoning beauty of fertility off in the distance. The good green earth!

A long, low-lying swatch of terrain, bordered with trees, mounted with tall grass of so brilliant and verdant a hue that it seemed to vie with the sunlight for sheer radiance. And luminosity.

His heart soared.

Behind him, Nova clawed at his back in confirmation of what his eyes had seen. Yes. This was where she had wanted to bring him. This was where Taylor might be. Or so he thought.

The horse now spurted forward, at a fast gallop, as if it too had been miraculously revivified by the change in the scenery ahead. Taking great strides, the beast plummeted forward, bouncing Brent and the girl in-discriminately. Brent didn't care. He couldn't quit the empty wasteland soon enough. He was leaving Hell behind.

The greener, richer country magnified in size, loom-ing large, larger, largest. Until it seemed to fill the whole new world. It was a fresh universe set down in the seeming middle of Nothingness. Brent rejoiced in his heart. He could tell the girl felt much better, too, by the manner in which her arms tightened around him as they drew even closer. He was unable to distinguish between fear and joy. Now, there were trees. A forest of them. Green and abiding. And thick copses of shrubbery. Hedges, measured landscaping. Like terraced gardens. The evident hand of a civilization of people. A land of green-thumbers who knew how to make things grow! Brent gave the horse its head but navigated it toward a trail cut directly into the heart of the pleasantly leafy outskirts of this oasis of beauty in a barren planet. There was hope yet . . .

The horse slowed, avoided overhanging boughs encroaching on the path and gingerly worked a passage among the verdant environs. Brent gave it free rein, but when Nova suddenly pulled at his uniform, he turned in bewilderment. She was indicating that they should both dismount and look first to see what they were getting into. It seemed a sensible idea. Brent slid off the horse and assisted the girl to the soft earth. Now, faintly, he could hear a mammoth roar. Like a distant thunder of waves beating against a shoreline. Puzzled, he allowed Nova to lead him where the bush was thickest. Here she tethered the horse so the animal could not run away. Then she joined the new white man and motioned for him to peer through the foliage in the direction of the strange cataract of sound. To Brent, unless the infernal heat he had suffered most of the day was making him hear things, the strange murmur of noise was like that of a large and vociferous crowd of people. At a stadium, say, or a political rally; like a convention.

Together, Brent and Nova crawled through the green shrubbery, found a vantage point and parted some overhead branches. Brent was the first to look. To goggle.

As he stared down toward the source of the waterfall of sound, his eyes bugged out, his mouth fell open and the scientific mind inside his skull did a pirouette of insanity.

"*My God——*" he blurted. "*A city of apes——!*"

It was true.

He was seeing what Taylor had seen way back at the beginning.

Seeing what Taylor had refused to believe until he had felt the first sting of a gorilla's whip and the first guttural commands of his ape jailers. Until he had lost all his comrades-in-space.

Seeing and daring not to believe, for it would mean that he was truly mad and had lost his mind when the spacecraft had come down in the desert in a crash landing.

He saw the complex of Ape City. The stone warrens, the dome-shaped houses, the granite walks and paths, the immense gorilla-house aspect of the kingdom which had sprung into being after Man had lost his way in the hierarchy of power. Below him he saw the circular stone arena in the heart of the city. Unbelievably, hundreds of apes were thronged there, standing together like any mass of humans who have come to hear someone speak. He could see squads of gorillas, uniformed like some kind of military personnel, brutally herding half-naked humans into wagon cages. The air was filled with the sounds of barked commands, cries of fright and pain. And something else Brent couldn't quite fathom. Not in his frenzy of fear and bewilderment.

"What are they doing to those people down there?" he almost begged the question of Nova. Behind him, crouching and remembering all too well, the girl did not answer. She couldn't.

At the arena's main gate, a picket-like arched entranceway, Brent could now see a small gathering of chimpanzees. Chimpanzees, armed with banners, walking around in circles, gesturing defiantly toward the center of the arena. The banners read: FREE THE HUMANS! UNITE IN PEACE! Nobody of the gorilla stamp was paying any attention to the dissenting chimpanzees. Brent shook himself, blinking. He was seeing things. He had to be—uniformed gorillas, chimps in civvies . . .

"This is a nightmare," he said huskily, mutely, his tongue thick in his mouth. His frantic eyes searched the arena dumbly.

He could feel Nova's hands trembling on his back. Nova, who still remembered the ordeal of Ape City. Brent was stupefied.

Nova was only—*afraid*.

4   URSUS

Down below on the perimeter of the stone arena, too far away for him to have spotted Brent and Nova in the concealment of thicket above, stood General Ursus. General Ursus had eyes only for the crowd. His audience. He stood on a dais, surrounded by the populace of Ape City, all eager to hear what he had to say—to offer. General Ursus was a very large, very imposing gorilla whose military costume of braid, epaulettes and medals merely enhanced the ferocity and brute strength of his appearance. Behind him on the dais, Nova would have recognized the elderly Dr. Zaius, the stern but kindly orangutan who had at least attempted to understand the freedom that Taylor had wanted and needed. Other members of the ape hierarchy filled the chairs ringed around the platform. But for the moment, the center of all eyes and ears was the mighty General Ursus.

Ursus the Powerful.
Ursus the Great One.

Even as he now spoke, holding out his long arms, his full-chested voice sweeping over the throngs, the great white statue of the Lawgiver behind him seemed to wrinkle in a smile of simian approval. Ursus was a man of the people.

"Greetings, members of the Citizens' Council," Ursus boomed. "I am a simple soldier——" Deafening applause and a wildly cheering multitude greeted this pronouncement. From the cover of the shrubbery above, Brent almost broke down in total astonishment. His eyes glittered insanely in his bronzed face. "*God, this is not real. It can't be—!*" Nova, terrified, pulled him back to cover.

"As a soldier," Ursus resumed, placidly, in control of his audience, "I see things simply——" His listeners had stilled, ready to absorb the rest of what he had to say.

Brent was talking to himself now, in a shattered whisper.

"I see an ape. He talks . . . ! I know what happened . . . Re-entry: twenty thousand miles an hour. A force of 15G. It made Skipper blind, and muddled my brains. So everything here is delusion—" he turned to Nova almost helplessly. "Even you—which is too bad . . ."

Nova, somehow understanding the horror of what had come to him, quickly placed her hand over his mouth.

The next words of Ursus came up to them, sonorous and clear. Like shining rocks aimed at what was left of Brent's sanity.

"What I saw, when I became your Army Commander, broke my heart. I saw our country imprisoned on one side by the sea, and by north and south and west—by naked desert. And inside our country, we found ourselves infected by those enormous parasites which we call *Humans*. By parasites who devoured the fruits that *we* had planted in a land rightly *ours;* who fattened on the fertility of fields that we had made green with wheat; who polluted the pure and precious water of *our* lakes and rivers with their animal excrement; and who continued to breed in our very midst like maggots in a once healthy body. What should we do? How should we act? I know what every soldier knows: the only thing that counts in the end is Power! Naked, merciless Force!" A low growl of applause filtered up from the crowd but no one was anxious to break the flow of Ursus' rhetoric.

"Today, the bestial Human herds have at last been systematically flushed from their feeding grounds! No single Human Being has escaped our net. They are dead. Or if not dead, they are in our cages——condemned to die."

The thick murmur flittering among his listeners began to swell into a low rumble, building to a full roar. Ursus smiled all too benignly. His deep-set eyes were as cold and cruel as leeches.

"I do not say that all Humans are evil," he declared, "simply because their skin is hairless. But our Lawgiver tells us that never will they have the Ape's divine faculty for distinguishing between Evil and Good. Their eyes are animal, their smell the smell of the dead flesh they eat. Had they been allowed to live and breed among us unchecked, they would have overwhelmed us. And the concept of Ape Power would have become meaningless; and our high and splendid culture would have wasted away and our civilization would have been ravaged and destroyed."

Now there was no holding the audience of apes, gorillas and camp followers. The stone arena thundered with noise. Ursus beamed down on a sea of simian faces. He raised his arms in gratitude and acknowledgment. From the hillside, Brent had listened with mounting horror and cold fury. Flat on their stomachs, he and the girl had worked themselves further away from the hideous tableau. Nova was shuddering as if she had palsy. Brent tried to steady her by holding her wrist firmly.

"I've got to get out," he told himself, trying to remain clearheaded. "And the only way out—is to take to the sky. I don't know how or what with—all I know is I can't stay here. If this place has a name, it's the Planet Nightmare . . ."

Backtracking furiously, slithering along the green earth like snakes, Brent and the shaking girl disappeared into the foliage.

Ursus had almost reached the end of his peroration. ". . . and those lucky enough to remain alive will have the privilege of being—*used*—" Here he half turned to bow slightly toward Dr. Zaius whose powerful face had remained inscrutable throughout the highly inflammatory speech, "by our revered Minister of Science, Dr. Zaius."

This last statement was uttered in a flat, unemphatic tone, but nevertheless a small but spirited outbreak of minority clapping sounded from the crowd below the dais, filling the arena. Dr. Zaius still did not smile, but Ursus frowned, flinging a furious glance toward an outer section of his audience.

He might have guessed. Zaius' advocates seemed to be the chimpanzee section of the crowd. The usual, typical kindly intellectuals who still used such expressions as the "milk of human kindness." What rot! Damn Zaius and all his intellectual weaklings! Ursus gestured peremptorily and a military policeman advanced on the section, brandishing his club. The clapping subsided. Except for one very energetic female chimpanzee who kept on clapping. Her companion, a male chimp, plucked at her sleeve nervously.

"Zira!" Cornelius whispered savagely. "Stop! You're in danger."

"So is the future of science with that rabble-rouser fomenting a senseless military adventure," his wife snorted angrily.

On the left flank of the crowd, in the concealment of the hillside, Nova had halted Brent. Pointing down toward the chimpanzee section, she gesticulated wildly toward Zira and Cornelius. Brent did not understand until Nova touched the ID disc around her throat and pointed back toward the arena. She had recognized Zira and Cornelius; two of the gentlest souls in this Ape City, who had helped her and Taylor effect their escape. The intelligent chimpanzees who in their long jackets and skirts and trousers had been like saints in a universe gone mad.

Ursus was winding up his oration.

"We will never lose our sense of purpose. We will never degenerate. We will never become weak and hairless—" Growls filtered up from his audience once more. "Because we know how to purify our own people——with *Blood!*"

His gimlet eyes swept over the dais, finding Dr. Zaius. Their glances locked. The conflict between the two of them hung like unexploded dynamite in the charged atmosphere.

"The Forbidden City," Ursus intoned heavily, "has been closed for centuries. And rightly so. But we now have evidence that that vast, barren area is now inhabited. By whom or by what, we do not know. But if they live—and live they do—then they must eat. We must replenish the land that was ravaged by the Humans with new, productive feeding grounds. And these we can obtain in the once Forbidden Zone. So now it is our holy duty to enter it, put the mark of our feet and wheels and guns and flags upon it! To *expand* the boundaries of our ineluctable power!"

A mammoth *a-a-a-ahhhhh!* erupted from the crowd.

"To kill our enemies—" Ursus thundered, shaggy

arms outflung, "known and unknown——like so many lice!"

A growl, a gathering crescendo of fury and might, swelled up from anthropoid throats. Ursus brought his arms down in a mighty sweep of finality, his voice climaxing the speech with one last fierce exhortation of brute force.

"And to invade—*invade*—INVADE, *INVADE!*"

The ranked gorillas, standing before the platform, blistered the air with applause. Hoarse shouts of exaltation rumbled wildly from the throng. With waves of acclaim cascading upon him, Ursus took a seat once more, his gorilla smile as wide as humility allowed. Dr. Zaius did not smile.

Seated and silent amid the uproar, the chimpanzee section of the audience sat in stunned despair. One Ursus, feeding flames to trigger-happy civilians, could fan a blaze that could wreck Ape City. Gorilla policemen, quick to put down troublemakers among the intellectuals, were circulating rapidly, wielding truncheons. And bayonets. The chimps who had refused to stand to honor Ursus and his speech were bullied into upright positions. All but Zira, who remained seated, her chimp muzzle screwed into an expression of defiance. Cornelius, standing to avoid a fight, was exceedingly perturbed by her foolhardiness.

"Zira!"

She wouldn't budge. Cornelius whispered to her in a fierce undertone.

"Zira, as your husband, I beg you to stand up."

"Only for my principles," she said clearly and coolly.

"All right," Cornelius smiled, in spite of himself. "For your principles then. And mine. Only *stand!*"

Zira dutifully got to her feet, a split second before a glowering gorilla policeman could reach her to force her to do so.

From the center of the arena, Ursus smiled a trium-

phant smile. No matter what the brainy fools might
think—force was the only answer for all problems.
Power. The Big Fist. *Ineluctable Power!*

Even his most vocal opposition, the chimpanzee
claque, were all on their feet now, paying homage to
what he had said. His words. His platform. His
promises.

Dr. Zaius would learn that someday, the scientific
idiot!

Or he too would have to feel a leather truncheon
crashing down on his orangutan skull.

Ursus knew that in his own scheme of things it could
be no other way.

Nova led the confused Brent through the thick un-
derbrush bordering Ape City. In her dimly lit mind
she had realized that perhaps Zira and Cornelius could
provide the new man with the answers she was incapable of giving. She had seen that Brent was the same
stamp of man as Taylor. There was the clean, bold look
of the eyes, the firm carriage of the body, the walk of
giants. Even if Brent was confused and obviously
dazed, to Nova he represented a species several thousand cuts above the half-savage, brutal race she had
grown and lived among. Anything was better than
that. Anything was better than the rule of apes.

The habitations were as she had remembered them.
Domelike huts and houses scaled on different levels of
the ground, terracing down like so many beehives. She
spotted Zira's home almost immediately. Brent tethered
the horse once again in the leafy undergrowth and they
proceeded on foot when she pointed out the way. Between the houses and huts, the brush was dense and
almost impenetrable. But it made concealment easier.
Brent stumbled along behind her, his mind still reeling
from the spectacle of the arena. Behind them, the
hoarse ovation for Ursus' speech still lingered in the

air. Nova suddenly halted as Brent came down too heavily on a twig beneath his heel. The noise cracked out clearly in the stillness of the brush. Nova pulled Brent to the soft earth.

A uniformed patrolman, his gorilla face savage beneath a visored cap, paused for a routine check. Through the density of foliage, Brent saw that they were only yards away from the guard. He held his breath, oddly terrified and bewildered. An ape in uniform walking around like any security policeman! With a weapon, too.

The gorilla cop was scanning the landscape with great care, trying to pin down the strange noise on his patrol. Crouching in the bushes, Nova and Brent lay very still. Suddenly there was an abrupt whirring noise. A bird, strangely multicolored, shot from a nearby thicket and whirled overhead. The patrolman quickly drew a heavy revolver from his belted holster and snapped off a shot. The bird was out of sight almost immediately, but Brent had to hold his teeth together to keep from screaming out loud. Nova's quick hand once more closed over his mouth as she saw the widening red stain on his shoulder. Brent closed his eyes against the sudden agony. The random shot had caught him as surely as if it had been aimed at him.

The patrolman, satisfied that the bird had been the source of the strange sound, holstered his pistol and continued on his way through the brush. His boots made clumping noises along the path.

Brent sagged against the earth, his face drawn with pain, as Nova bent over him helplessly.

From the distant arena, heavy shouts again filled the air.

The steam room, banked benches of stone nearly obscured by the rising clouds of vapor, was the scene of an important conference. A little gorilla boy, busily ladling cold water over the hissing hot stones, might have been a statue devoid of life. Dr. Zaius and General Ursus had repaired here to discuss the important issues evoked by the open forum in the arena of Ape City.

Lolling in loincloths, ministered to by the gorilla boy, Zaius and Ursus were airing their views (and their differences) in a more intimate and unguarded atmosphere. Sometimes, disparate minds may meet in private where they cannot come together in public.

Zaius fervently hoped so. His reddish-blond orangutan coloring was in marked contrast to Ursus' jet black, shaggier gorilla proportions. Both apes liked the steam room. It was a good place to sweat out differences and divergences of opinion.

"General Ursus," Zaius suggested, "I can only pray that you know what you are doing."

Ursus shrugged his mammoth shoulders, sweat trickling down off his snout of a nose.

"How can you doubt it, Dr. Zaius, after the reports we have been receiving of strange manifestations in the Forbidden Zone? Manifestations which you, as Minister of Science, have been unable to fathom. Twelve of my scouts have vanished into thin air."

"Eleven," Zaius reminded him, with his fetish for exactitude.

"*Eleven.* And the twelfth came back with incredible reports of huge walls of fire and strange earthquakes. His mind was shattered—undoubtedly by some unSimian torture."

"Inflicted by whom?"

"Who knows? but they live. Therefore they eat."

"I still think you are being—hasty."

"No," Ursus snorted mightily. "Decisive!"

Dr. Zaius shook his head.

"Decisions come from weighing evidence. It is through evidence that a scientist arrives at the truth."

"And a politician?"

"At expediency."

For a long, crucial second, both apes regarded each other eye to eye. The steaming vapors swirled and eddied about them. General Ursus chuckled almost softly.

"Then let us discuss what is evident and what is expedient. What is evident is that by this overpopulation, we face famine. What is expedient is . . ."

". . . that we should control it," Dr. Zaius interjected quickly.

Ursus glared. His nostrils quivered.

"And be outnumbered by our enemies? I look to the day when not thousands but millions will march under the Ape banner."

"Should we not wait until then, if we must invade?"

"And let our enemies invade us first?" Ursus wagged his mighty head. "I would sooner attack at *my* convenience than be forced to defend at theirs. We invade or we starve. It's as simple as that."

"And as dangerous," Zaius said slowly.

Ursus frowned at his gentle foe, barely concealing the wrathful scorn he felt for all thinkers such as the eminent doctor.

"What is more dangerous than famine?" he demanded, almost shouting. The little gorilla boy paused dumbly in his labors.

"The unknown," Dr. Zaius said.

Steam rose and hissed over the hot rocks as the cold water hit them, seeming to fan the atmosphere with the import of Dr. Zaius' warning.

General Ursus could only glare anew.

Words of wisdom.

Intellectual thin-skinnedness.

Psychological hogwash.

Cowardice. Anything to avoid direct action or confrontation! It was no more than he expected from the likes of Dr. Zaius.

5   ZIRA AND CORNELIUS

En route from the dissatisfying public display of sentiment at the arena, Zira paused on the threshold of her home to give further vent to her chagrin. Cornelius, dutifully following behind her, allowed her to continue. He had learned a long time ago that in dealing with a female, a male has no recourse but to give her tongue free rein. Cornelius was a very intelligent young chimpanzee, as well as a scientist. He also set great store by Zira's intellect—and heart.

Zira was still fuming in an undertone as they reached the front door of their habitat.

"If I had any sense of scientific purpose, Cornelius, I shouldn't be cutting up the healthy heads of humans. I should be dissecting the diseased brains of gorillas to find out what went wrong."

Cornelius smiled. "And how would you put it right?"

He opened the door for her but she paused, striking herself on the breast. Her cute little face was puckered up in a scowl.

"Wet-nurse their babies on the milk of chimpanzees. The milk of kindness. At least when *our* child is born, it won't be breast-fed on bile."

Cornelius chuckled and pushed her gently into their house. Zira flounced in, still angry, heading for the kitchen. Cornelius took off his shoes, settled himself in an easy chair and groped for his pipe. The interior of their home never failed to fill him with a sense of comfort and well-being. They had wooden table and chairs, framed pictures included the gilt portrait of the two of them on their wedding day. An open archway in the living room led into Zira's kitchen where she cooked and baked so many fine things. All in all a very domestic hideout for a pair of chimpanzee scientists. Cornelius sighed, thinking about that and what Zira had said, as he sat back in his worn old chair.

"The trouble with us intellectuals, my dear," he said as he filled his clay pipe, "is that we have responsibility but no power."

Zira didn't answer him. She had already put on her white apron, taken out a China bowl and a box of ready-mix, and with a fork was stirring up some sort of batter. He could already smell the ingredients of something.

"I think I'll make chocolate icing. Do you like chocolate? No—you don't. Well, I do . . ."

Cornelius frowned. Perhaps she hadn't heard him. He tried again.

"And if we did take power into our hands, we'd be as bad, or worse, than *Them*."

She'd heard him, all right. Mixing furiously, her next words had absolutely nothing to do with chocolate icing.

"I don't agree. They're a genetic accident. A mistake of nature. The gorillas are cruel because they're stupid. All bone and little brain . . ."

"Ssshh!" Cornelius begged. "My dear. I wish you wouldn't talk like that. Somebody may hear you."

Zira snorted and Cornelius sighed in despair.

It was at this precise moment that Nova emerged from the tiny curtained alcove to the left of the living room. Behind her, Brent swayed, tall and shadowy in the dimness of the aperture. Nova stood stock-still, her eyes fastened on Zira, hoping for the best.

"Nova!" Zira blurted, as if she had seen a ghost.

Cornelius came up out of his chair, as startled as his wife.

"What are you doing here?"

Knowing the girl could not speak, Zira's eyes went to the figure of Brent whose face she could not yet identify in the shadows.

"Taylor—" she began, a sound of hope in her voice.

"My name isn't Taylor," Brent spoke up. "It's Brent." He stepped into the light of the room. But Zira and Cornelius had recoiled, almost as if he had struck them. They were doing a double take of wonder.

"You talked!" Zira gasped, looking around the room as if she expected some sort of trick.

"Impossible," Cornelius agreed.

Zira stared at Brent. Her tiny eyes marveled. She shook her head, Nova almost forgotten in this fresh miracle.

"In a whole lifetime devoted to the scientific study of humans, I've found only one other like you who could talk."

Brent nodded. "Taylor," he said. His eyes roved the room, fearful.

"Taylor!" Cornelius echoed. "Is he alive? Have you seen him?"

"Where?" Zira pleaded. "Where? Tell us!"

Brent stared at them, still everlastingly confounded by the image of apes who could speak English as plain as he could. But he was adjusting. If this was lunacy, then so be it. They were all at least on the same wave length. Talking about Taylor—there *was* something reassuring about that, mad as it was.

"I don't know where," he faltered. "I'm trying to find him and the longer I'm here, the less I'm beginning to care." He held his hand against his damaged shoulder, wincing. Nova hung back, staring at the people who could talk, but somehow looking happy that things were being accomplished. Brent smiled at her, faintly.

"We loved Taylor," Cornelius said proudly. "He was a fine, a unique specimen."

Brent reacted to that almost violently. His face flew from Cornelius to Zira and then to Cornelius again.

"And if it had not been for Zira," Cornelius continued passionately, "he'd be here still—a stuffed specimen, with glass eyes, in the Great Hall of the Zaius Museum. Like his two friends."

"Like his two friends," Brent echoed slowly, suddenly realizing the monstrous truth of what had happened to Taylor and the others if all that he had seen and heard was true. "I don't plan to stay quite that long. Look, can you give us some food, water, and a map, so I know where I'm going."

Zira nodded, looking at his red-stained shoulder.

"Your arm also needs some care." Without another word, she went out through the curtained doorway.

"I'll get the map." Cornelius walked to a cabinet in one corner, plucked a rolled scroll of paper from it and brought it back to the table where he spread it out for Brent's examination. Nova hovered at Brent's shoulder, silent, wide-eyed. Cornelius, his brows beetled in concentration, began to explain the curious red and blue markings on the map. Brent was fascinated.

"Here is our city. And here, to the north, is where Zira and I . . ."

His wife had come back, laden down with a cloth, water pitcher, a bowl, forceps and sticking plaster. As Cornelius continued, Zira deftly began to treat Brent's shoulder. When she sprinkled the wound with some sort of powder, Brent gasped. The powder stung.

"What's that damn stuff you're using?" he barked.

"You wouldn't know if I told you," she said placidly. "Just relax. Among other things, I'm a trained vet."

"Thanks," Brent apologized. "Go on, go on . . ."

Cornelius indicated the map. "We last saw Taylor with Nova going through the gap between this lake and the sea." He pointed. Brent saw the spot and nodded. A dot in that hellish wasteland . . .

Zira said, "They were heading deep into the territory we call . . ."

"Yes, yes—I know," Brent said. "The Forbidden Zone."

For a moment, there was a pindrop of silence. Then Zira finished dressing Brent's wound, putting the bandage into place. Her face was expressionless. Only her eyes held a glow.

"Who told you that?" she asked.

"Your glorious leader back there." Brent jerked his good shoulder in the direction of the arena.

Before Zira could respond, there was a knock on the front door of the house. Everybody stiffened, right where they stood. Then, as the knocking became louder, there was sudden activity. Cornelius jumped for the map on the table, Brent moved back to the curtained alcove, Zira hustled the petrified Nova in the same direction. She drew the curtains and shut them both in, out of sight. Cornelius rolled up the map quickly, taking it back to the cabinet. Zira calmly straightened out her skirt. "Open the door, Cornelius," she said.

"But—" he indicated the medical apparatus, frightened.

"Open it."

Cornelius spread his hands and did as she told him.

Dr. Zaius came bounding into the room, walking springily for an ape of his great years. His shrewd old face was furrowed with sternness. There was an air of great urgency about him.

"Dr. Zaius!" Cornelius stammered. "We were just going to eat . . ."

Zaius brushed by him, wagging a cane.

"Not before I've talked some sense into that head-strong wife of yours. Where is she?"

"Well—she's . . ."

Desperately, Cornelius turned. He was shocked to find Zira lying down on the divan, which was located near all the medical apparatus. He blinked. Zaius blustered by him, going toward Zira on the couch. The cane clumped along the floor.

"Good day, Dr. Zaius," Zira said wanly.

Zaius stopped fuming, concern immediately etching his face.

"What happened? Has there been an accident?"

Zira sat up. Suddenly it was clear that a large patch of sticking plaster was affixed to her right cheek. A fresh one.

"Cornelius hit me," Zira said.

Her husband gaped down at her, openmouthed.

"For my bad behavior at the meeting," Zira explained to the good doctor. She seemed almost contrite.

Zaius grunted. "I don't blame him."

Zira nodded. "I don't resent it." She touched the plaster gingerly. "But his nails need clipping."

Cornelius stifled his outrage but Dr. Zaius had already put the family quarrel behind him. He waved his cane angrily.

"Enough of this nonsense! Are you so blind, you two psychologists, that you are unaware that we are on the brink of a grave crisis? You heard the Ursus speech . . ."

"Militaristic tripe!" growled Zira, her old self again.

"Sh-h-h!" Cornelius begged, agonized.

"Perhaps," Zaius said evenly, studying Zira. "But eleven of his gorilla scouts, on reconnaissance in the Forbidden Zone, have vanished . . ."

"Well, it serves him right," Zira said huffily.

"Zira," Cornelius pleaded, once again, for reason, not

feminine contrariness; it was an old song to Dr. Zaius.

"And Ursus," he continued, "is determined to have his revenge. All-out war if need be." Turning, he walked to the table. His reddish-haired body shone in the light of the room.

"Ursus now has the 'incident' he needs to go on a rampage of conquest." He looked at the tip of his heavy wooden cane.

Cornelius started. "But that is appalling! When Zira and I first unlocked the secrets of the Forbidden Zone, you intervened at our trial for heresy."

"I know."

"The price we paid for our freedom was the vow to you never to disclose our discovery that Man evolved from the Ape . . ."

"But to remain silent," Zira interrupted, "while this bully, Ursus, is permitted to destroy everything in his path, is no longer possible."

Dr. Zaius' face looked suddenly older as he fixed his gaze on his younger colleagues.

"You want to stand trial once more for heresy? No, my children, this time I may not be here to plead for clemency."

Zira looked worried. "Where are you going?"

"Into the Forbidden Zone with Ursus."

Zira's expression changed to one of scorn, unhidden.

"Another manhunt, Doctor?"

Zaius was not unaware of her feelings. Or her convictions.

"The disappearance of these scouts is more than the work of a mere man. Some*one* or some*thing* has outwitted the intelligence of the gorillas."

Zira snorted. "That shouldn't be difficult."

"Zira," Cornelius groaned. "Please . . ."

Zaius ignored her.

"As Minister of Science, it is my duty to find out whether some other form of life exists. Some new threat to our ape civilization. Before Ursus barges in and destroys the evidence."

Zira shook Cornelius off. "But if these creatures, or whatever they are, are so intelligent, why shouldn't they be able to live with us in peace and harmony?"

"For the same reasons," Zaius said, wearily almost, for he had argued the very point with Zira so many times, "that man could not live in harmony, even with his own kind. He abused his own intelligence and destroyed his own world. We apes have learned to live in innocence. Let no one, be he man or some other creature, attempt to corrupt that innocence." When he saw the smirk on Zira's face, he bridled. "Why? Is innocence so evil?"

"Ignorance is," Zira said firmly.

"There is a *time* for truth," Dr. Zaius said sternly.

"And the time is always now," Zira reminded him.

Dr. Zaius stared at her.

"Bah!" he exploded, thumping his cane on the wooden floor. Cornelius shuddered, closing his eyes.

Zira shook her head. "Are you asking me to surrender my principles?"

Dr. Zaius frowned. But his eyes were kindly, glittering.

"I am asking you to be the guardians of the higher principles of science in my absence. I am asking for a truce with your personal convictions in an hour of public danger."

"And you shall have it," Cornelius interposed strongly, brooking no protest from Zira. "Or I—shall hit her again, Dr. Zaius."

"Let's have no violence, Cornelius," Zaius muttered as he moved toward the door. "Now, I'm relying on you both."

"And we're relying on you, too," Zira reminded him, getting the last shot in.

Dr. Zaius paused on the threshold of their house.

"If I should fail to return from the Unknown, the whole future of our civilization will be yours to preserve—or destroy. So think well before you act."

"Goodbye, Doctor," Zira said, warmly enough, "and good luck."

From their wide window they watched him patter down the walk until his familiar figure was out of sight, cane and all. Cornelius heaved a sigh of gratitude and then went to the alcove to summon the girl and Brent out of hiding. Zira was contemplative, thinking over what Dr. Zaius had said. He had looked and sounded so tired . . .

Brent was white-faced and weak. Nova held on to him, close at his side. Zira stirred herself.

"Come on, let me finish this and get you out of here."

"Yes," Brent growled. "Get me out of here—please. I've seen the delicate, 'humane' way they treat humans around here. I don't much care for it." He took Nova's hand and squeezed it.

"Have you a horse?" Zira asked.

"Up in the scrub," Brent admitted.

"I'll have to get you another set of clothes—the kind fit for humans like yourself. You'll pass. And get rid of this."

She pointed to his ID tags. She went to Nova and removed Taylor's tags from her throat.

"And get rid of this too—" But Nova grabbed the tags back, belligerently almost. Zira shrugged.

"If you are caught by the gorillas," Cornelius offered, "remember one thing."

"What's that?" Brent demanded.

"Never to speak."

"What the hell would I have to say to a gorilla?"

"But you don't understand," Cornelius protested. "Only apes can speak. If they catch you speaking, they will dissect you. And they will kill you. In that order."

The irony of such a proposition did not escape Brent, tired and confused as he was. He grinned wearily.

Zira had returned with the human clothing which she passed on to Brent. He was not surprised to find it no more than rags; a pitiful loincloth and smocklike thing. But he took them all the same. He wasn't so stupefied that he couldn't recognize kindness when he found it. These two chimps were Okay Joes.

"Cornelius is right," Zira agreed. "Be very careful and get out of those things you are wearing as soon as you can."

Brent nodded, arms full, took Nova by the hand and led her to the door of the house. There he stopped and turned.

"Thanks," he said, simply. It was all he could think of to say. He had never had hospitality from an ape before.

"Thank us by finding Taylor," Zira said softly, a light shining from deep within her gimlet eyes.

"If he's alive," Brent said.

There was no more to be said.

He left, taking Nova with him.

Leaving behind Zira and Cornelius to ponder again the remarkable peculiarity of humans who could speak.

The Lawgiver would have revolved on his stone base if word of that had ever come to him.

The figure of a Great Ape reading a book would not have understood—or believed—such a phenomenon.

He who was supposed to know all things.

6   NOVA

Brent and Nova did not get very far.

As soon as he had changed from his astronaut's white into the ragged remnants of what passed for human clothing, both he and the girl struck out through the scrub in the direction of the Forbidden Zone. The brush was quiet, almost tropical, with nothing but the occasional twitter of winged creatures indicating any form of activity. The sun still held the heavens, raining down an unremitting liquid sunshine. The glare was almost unbearably bright. Brent had to keep his eyes continually slitted. Nova seemed not to mind. Together, very cautiously, she and Brent worked a route through the trees and bushes. Once they had retrieved the horse, Brent hurriedly mounted up, swinging Nova on behind him.

They moved as fast as the terrain would allow.

Brent kept the horse at a careful trot, eyes peeled for trouble. The girl clung to him, her lithe body almost a part of his own. Any other time, any other place, it would have been an extraordinarily pleasant sensation, but not now. Brent's mind was far too filled with the horror of Ape City to heed it.

His consciousness, his mentality, was too busy fighting off an assault of total unreality. The crash landing, the Time jump, Skipper's death, the remarkable news about Taylor—all of it had made his sanity teeter precariously toward complete incoherence. His brain was filled with pictures and images of apes talking, apes acting like doctors, apes rolling up and reading maps . . .

But he pushed the horse on, the soldier in him still on duty. The habits of a lifetime are hard to break.

When the single rifle shot cracked out and the horse beneath him suddenly reeled in a headlong plunge to the earth, he responded almost like an automaton. The air blazed with more gunfire and then he was vaguely aware of himself and the girl, up and running; breaking like startled rabbits for the nearest cover. He heard Nova cry out in fear. His mind was perforated with frenzy. He ran madly, pulling the girl, trying to see from which point the danger came. And then time and place overwhelmed him. And doom.

Gorillas were charging them from all points of the compass. Armed gorillas, brandishing truncheons, pointing rifles. Leather-jacketed troops of some insane sort of militia. They bounded in closer and Brent whirled to fight. His eyes bulged in terror. He could now smell the zoolike aura of their bodies, could almost see the fierce intelligence in their beady black eyes. Nova screamed again. Brent struck out wildly, burying his fist on a simian snout. But they closed in on him and the girl. A swarm of brute force. Helmeted, uniformed, and oddly silent and efficient. Brent went down under a weight of bodies. Coarse, leathery hands raked him. Gorilla claws plucked at his flesh. He tried to lash out, kick away, but he was borne to the soft earth, his nostrils filled with the singular stink of defeat. His mind clouded over. They were spread-eagling him on the ground, as helpless as any chicken with a wolf pack. A rough leather collar with a long, trailing leash was slung around his neck. Nova was being similarly manhandled. Gorilla-handled? Brent strove to laugh at the bitter irony of the whole situation. But he couldn't. His throat was like ashes. The gorilla smell and the gorilla might boxed in his senses like an awesome reversal of all the norms in any man's universe.

Low growls and snorts emanated from his captors. But no words. Which somehow only made it worse.

The militia of gorillas led Brent and Nova away, dragging them by the long leashes off through the scrub toward—what?

Brent did not even want to speculate.

All he could remember and think of until it burned like a hot poker in his skull was Cornelius' warning: *Never speak. If they catch you speaking, they will dissect you. And then they will kill you. In that order.*

There was no danger of Nova speaking.

Brent only fully realized the extent of his predicament when he and Nova were literally hurled through the gates of a human pen and the barred doors swung shut. It took only one look to understand to what incredible degree Man had fallen and the Ape had risen.

For here, locked up in wooden cages, were dozens of humans. Emaciated to the point of starvation, filthy, festered with sores, some of them howling like wild dogs, some of them dying, some of them possibly already dead. All in all, a thoroughly hopeless and helpless amalgam of savagery, stupidity and total ignorance of man's basic superiority to his ape jailers.

Nova shrank against Brent in one corner of the horrible cage, trembling. Brent tried to hang on to his nerve. It wasn't easy.

The awful stench of the place, the terrible sight of the gorilla guards on duty beyond the barred walls, was enough to drive a sane man right out of his mind. What was left of it.

But Brent kept his lips closed, trying not to cry out, in the name of God and science, for help.

He remembered what Cornelius had told him.

He would have to wait.

The horrors mounted.

No more than an hour later, two horse-drawn cage

wagons, each driven by a gorilla teamster, clattered up outside their filthy pen. Brent felt a ray of hope. For standing outside their cage was Cornelius! Cornelius in his long coat and trousers, busy with pad and pencil. With him was an armed gorilla guard. And unless he was hearing things, Cornelius was in the process of selecting humans for research! The regular guards were manhandling at least six of the wretched human tide into one of the carts, acting obviously on Cornelius' instructions. There was a great howling and resistance put up by the humans, but effective slashes of rubber truncheons and leather whips were making the fight pitifully inadequate. Cornelius displayed no emotion at this. Brent grit his teeth, hanging onto Nova. There was so much he couldn't understand.

A sergeant rode up, his three stripes glowing in the glare of sunlight. The gorilla face was a mockery beneath billed cap. The sergeant barked at the guard with Cornelius: "Twenty required on Number Two Range for C Company target practice. Jump to it!"

Now more humans were thrust into the two cage-carts. Brent and Nova were manhandled out of the pen, pushed toward the first waiting cart. But suddenly Cornelius seemed to spot them and came forward, holding up a delaying paw. The guards holding Brent and the girl waited for his instructions.

"Stop a minute," Cornelius said coolly.

He approached Brent, his face without expression, and appraised the face before him. He jabbed his fingers into Brent's jawbone, explored his cranium. Brent strove to maintain a calm he didn't feel. Then Cornelius lifted Nova's eyelid, all the while murmuring some impressive medical gibberish. As if musing half aloud to himself.

"Brachycephalic—*and* prognathous . . . incipient glaucoma . . . hmmm." He raised his voice, for the guards' benefit. "We could do with these two." He signaled for Brent and Nova to be put aside for further examination and study.

The mounted sergeant spurred closer, his tone surly and insolent. And impatient. His right hand bore a menacing truncheon.

"Required for human target practice on Number Two Range," he repeated. "Captain Odo's orders."

Cornelius stared up at him icily.

"Required for cranial research by order of Dr. Zaius, Minister of Science." With that, he turned to the guards and indicated the second wagon. "Load them up."

The sergeant snarled, but whipped his horse around angrily and trotted off. Brent and Nova now found themselves hustled into the second cage-cart. The door clanged shut behind them. Up front, the gorilla driver cracked his whip. The wagon rolled forward. Brent stared through the bars of the cage at Cornelius. But Cornelius had returned to his study and examination of the rest of the filthy pack remaining in the big human pen. Business as usual! Once more, Brent could only muffle his astonishment and anger. He was perplexed.

Nor did the wagon journey through the streets of Ape City lessen his aggravation. Through the bars, with the silent Nova ever just behind him, he witnessed even more of the spectacle of a world gone topsy-turvy. A universe insane. As they made for the out-skirts of the complex, he could see many signs of some kind of military preparations: apes in close-order drill, apes taking courses in the use of the bayonet, apes stabbing dummies made up to resemble humans, apes going through the paces of rifle instruction. Ape City —if all the evidence was to be trusted—seemed to be making ready for some invasion or *sortie*. Was the city under siege? Had the humans somehow gotten back to their former level and threatened the apes with total extinction? It was too much to hope for.

Brent sank wearily to the floor of the cart. His shoulder hurt again, his eyes were like two blazing balls of fried meat, his mind was coming apart. Nova huddled against him, her eyes wide open and oddly tranquil, despite their plight. Perhaps it was an old story to her, the only thing she had ever known—being pushed around by gorillas. For Brent, it would never be easy to take.

Still, what was there he could do about it?

Now, at least.

Yet there was something hopeful, something to think about, as his eyes watched the gorillas mounting artillery field pieces and grooming horses for combat. The view did not change one iota on all the long, harrowing trip toward the outskirts of Ape City.

Something was up.

At the Research Complex, Dr. Zaius' own special kingdom, there was also much activity, if of a different kind. Zaius himself had invited General Ursus down to see what was going on. The Gorilla, massive and impressive as always in his uniform and medals, was walking around the compound inspecting the experimental cages and devices which formed the nucleus of Zaius' work. Zira was also on the scene. With a chimpanzee assistant at her elbow, she was accepting the newest delivery of cage-wagon humans sent from the city proper by her husband Cornelius. Zaius and Ursus, strolling the compound now for a chat, had just come into view when the gorilla driver delivered his wagonload of specimens which included Brent and Nova. The human cargo was as wretched as ever.

Zira, withholding her shock, approached Brent and Nova very casually. She had not expected to see them again so soon.

Brent held his ground. There was nothing else he could do.

Zira stared up at him.

"Male. Type E cranium. Very unusual." The chimpanzee at her elbow rapidly made some notes on her pad.

Zira reached up, tweaked Brent's ear and gave him a deliberately deadpan wink that only he could see.

"Weak occipital development. Substandard lobes—" She turned her attention to Nova who was staring at her dumbly. "Female. Type—" She broke off, for now she could see Dr. Zaius and General Ursus walking toward her. The sight disturbed her. Zaius was saying, ". . . so be it. You know that my scruples were dictated by caution—not by cowardice. When the day comes, I shall ride with you." Ursus was grunting a reply, but his piggish eyes were roving over Brent and Nova with undue interest. Zira quickened her routine survey, anxious to be gone. The guards were impatient too.

"It's been a long time since we've been able to study specimens of such extraordinary clinical interest," Zira said too loudly. "Take them inside . . ."

"You can't have them," General Ursus suddenly spoke up behind her. Zira whirled.

General Ursus' ugly face was wreathed in what passed for a smile. A horsewhip was coiled in his huge right paw.

"They've been marked," he explained quietly, "for target practice." As he said this, he flicked the whip and it cut cruelly across Nova's lithe body. Brent flinched but held his silence. General Ursus had already turned away, leading Dr. Zaius off with him. Zira raged inwardly. The gorilla driver, now that his leader had spoken, needed no second urging; he was already pushing Brent and the girl toward his cage-wagon. The vehicle was empty now, its desperate occupants removed for further research. The door at the rear hung open. Zira helped the driver to force Brent and Nova into the van. Brent moved like a dead man. This last had been too much for him. All the fight had gone out of him. He was dead-tired and dead-hopeless. As the driver went about his paces, Zira locked the cage door. Brent sat down on the floor of the wagon, his head in his hands. Nova began to weep. Softly and terribly. Brent was suddenly galvanized. He jumped to his feet, shaking the bars of the cage, his face furious. The cords in his neck stood out with the effort. Nova, with uncomprehending obedience, stopped crying and followed suit. Together they made a pitiful sight. Humans rattling the bars of their cage.

Brent wildly pointed to the lock of the cage door. Zira nodded as the driver returned to the front seat of his wagon. Her cute chimpanzee face was almost kindly.

"These poor animals," she said so that the driver could hear her. "They think blind force is the answer to everything."

The driver grunted, and reached for his whip.

"Wait—I'll double-lock the door," Zira said.

Under cover of the clatter of the wagon rolling once more into motion, Zira took out her key and *unlocked* the door of the cage, but without opening it. Brent stared at her.

"Good luck," she whispered.

He kept on staring at her, dumbly, long after the driver's whip had spurred the horses into a steady trot, long after her simian figure in its outlandish skirt and jacket was a solitary speck in the dust of the roadway. The motionless figure of Zira was a sight that Brent would always remember. For whatever was left of his life.

He could not account for the lump of something in his throat, nor for the fact that his eyes had filled with tears.

Zira's milk of kindness had engulfed him.

The wagon rumbled along at a good clip, heading back to the city, and Brent waited for the proper time to make his move. He had to pick a convenient moment. The terrain was still alive with ape preparations for war. They passed a cavalry of gorillas maneuvering in an intricate pattern that brooked no good for any foe ever caught by it. So Brent waited, biding his time, comforting Nova, who in her eternal speechlessness was never more than a senseless receptacle for all the ill that came her way. Brent's heart had gone out to her almost from the beginning. Her appeal was enormous. Apart from her physical attributes, she was like some lost and forlorn child you wanted to hold in your arms to make her stop crying, stop being afraid. God knew he was terrified himself. Scared virtually spitless, to put it baldly, truthfully.

But a man had to fight to survive.

Something the apes should always have realized.

Their own loss if they hadn't.

So Brent waited until the proper moment should come.

It did.

The driver had led the wagon through a stretch of deserted terrain, asprinkle with trees and shrubs, and it was here that Brent found his spot for an escape plan.

With Nova silently waiting, he opened the cage door, swung out over the roadway and clambered atop the wagon's roof. The gorilla head of the driver, hunched over his reins, was visible just above the forward lip of the cage. Brent edged forward on his hands and knees, mindful of the jarring passage of the wagon along the bumpy roadway. His hands tightened about the long leather leash trailing from his dog collar. His eyes were not quite sane as he reached the driver. Then he jumped. Like a savage who knows that it is the victim's death or his own. The gorilla head jerked violently. Great paws came up, fighting the hands from behind that were garroting with the leather leash. Brent was remorseless. He put all his mad weight into his arms and twisted savagely until the gorilla slumped lifelessly against his body. Brent stepped down and kicked the driver's inert form out of the seat. When the body hit the roadway, disappearing in the wagon dust, Brent could have screamed in exaltation. Even killing felt fine and good in this godawful place!

Like getting some of your own back.

With the fever singing in his veins, he drew the horses to a halt. There was no time to lose. They couldn't run around this infernal country in an open wagon. Not one of *their* wagons, at any rate.

Brent cut the two horses loose with a knife he found on a rack in the driver's seat. Then he went back to see about Nova, but she had already jumped out of the cage to join him. Her eyes were excited but still frightened. He patted her hand, motioned to the horses, keeping a wary eye on their surroundings for any signs of the gorilla cavalry. They weren't out of the woods yet. It was far too early to send up any skyrockets or do victory jigs.

This land still belonged to the Almighty Ape.

Quickly they mounted the horses and galloped away. It might have been Brent's imagination but he would have sworn he could hear a great hullaballoo starting up behind them. As if their escape on horseback had been spotted, as if it was already known that two humans had outwitted their gorilla captor. Brent didn't dare turn around and look. He had had enough of horror and fear in one day to last him a lifetime. Two lifetimes, in or out of the Hasslein Curve in the bend of Time. Now he only wanted out—the sooner the better.

He kept galloping his horse until the terrain became extremely rocky, stacked with gigantic boulders that towered as tall as buildings. Nova remained as close behind him as possible. He was ever conscious of her long-haired figure just out of reach. Whatever she was, the girl was a skillful rider, having no difficulty at all keeping up with him. Brent was grateful for that, too. He needed somebody to hold his own hand, never mind his being the only shoulder to lean on.

The high rocks loomed before them.

The sun was going down, hiding behind a shelf of ledge that seemed to fill the world. Blood-red rays tinged the landscape.

Brent rode on.

So did the girl.

Turning and twisting their mounts, they sought to find a passage between the mighty rock upheaval spread before them. A forest of stone.

They were blocked now by what must have been a recent landslide of earth and rock. The horses shied, whinnying, fighting for a level flooring for their hooves. Dismayed, Brent ordered the girl to dismount, for they could navigate now only on foot. That was obvious. No horse could have found a path through this obstacle of rock and stone and earth. There was no definable trail.

Brent and Nova found an opening between the boulders and the rocky obstacles. Stumbling and staggering, the horses behind them, they found their thorny path leading them to a shallow stream of running water. Around them on all sides the great rocks sprung like monolithic giants in a wilderness of stone.

Not too far behind them, peering from the crest of the high rock shelf, a ring of silhouetted apes watched the man and the woman work their way along the stream between the boulders.

The gorilla militia looked down, their helmeted heads and hunched shoulders menacing and unreal in the half light now darkening the planet of the apes. Their rifles and bayonets gleamed.

Brent and Nova had reached the Forbidden Zone.
A part of it, at least, where no gorilla dared tread.
Or could.
Without risking the disasters of the *Unknown*.

7   BRENT AND NOVA

They had emerged from the maze of rocks.

To Brent it was like walking into two thousand years
of time. He had to blink against the unreality of what
he now saw. What Nova must be seeing, though the
girl couldn't possibly have understood any of it. For
Brent it was the single act of entering a long tunnel.
He strained his eyes to see, to comprehend. But he
couldn't. He had stepped into a tableau from which
there was no withdrawing. He had stepped into Yester-
day—and what was worse, he had also stepped into
Tomorrow. The Tomorrow he had never known.

He and Nova were in an underground subway
station.

There was no mistake.

Slivers of gray daylight filtered feebly through dark
upper gratings, dimly illuminating the long, corroded
tracks stretching ahead between damp, glistening platforms. The stone and wood of the platforms were
cracked and fissured with age.

Brent was too stunned to speak. Nova trailed along
behind the barrier of his body. Brent could only stare
all about him, trying to adjust to the shock of some
indubitable truth struggling to make itself known to his
intelligence.

He began to walk, like a somnambulist, conscious only of a *drip, drip, dripping* sound somewhere. Like water falling eternally on stone. The walls above the platforms, ancient, rotting, now revealed a pitiful sign of some kind. Brent ran his fingers along the wet, scummy wall, walking hypnotically, following the steady rhythm of *drip, drip, drip.* Nova followed him. Brent paused. The texture of the wall had subtly changed. Brent stared up the wall, at the sign. It mocked his sanity and his reason:

QUEENSBOROUGH PLAZA

The *drip, drip, drip* sounded very near now. Brent craned his neck higher.

A glittering stalactite, dangling from the vaulted roof of the subway cavern, looked as sharp as any sword. Brent shuddered, his eyes falling away. Until he saw another rust-eaten sign: NEW YORK IS A SUMMER FESTIVAL. And further on, another: KEEP YOUR SUBWAY CLEAN. Until, at floor level, he saw row upon row of menacing, cold stalagmites. Brent stared from the signs to the stalagmites, his courage dissolving. This wasn't a subway, it was a cave—a hall of a mountain king where you'd expect to find trolls and witches and warlocks—! His senses reeled.

"God Almighty!" his voice crackled hollowly in the empty, dead tunnel. "This was my home! I lived and worked here once! What happened? Did we finally do it? Did we finally really do it?"

His voice rang off the barren lifeless walls. There was no answer for him. Just as there hadn't been for Taylor.

"What does a man do when he comes home—and there is no home?" He shook his head in disbelief as his own question echoed foolishly in his own ears. Then quietly, trying to absorb this incredible unreality, he turned to Nova, who could only stare back at him in confusion, not knowing what he was thinking or feeling.

"It's a damn nightmare!" Brent shouted at her, letting go. "A damn nightmare——a damn nightmare!"

Nova, seeing his misery, timidly touched his face.

The long subterranean labyrinth echoed and re-echoed with his cries of frustration.

The temple was small and austere. It was exactly in the center of Ape City. There was no altar. Against a plain backdrop of stone stood the revered statue of the Lawgiver. The Great Ape was still holding his book for all Time itself. Below the idol stood an orangutan minister, clad in scarlet. Before him, listening to his invocation, knelt Dr. Zaius, General Ursus and the balance of the ape hierarchy. Like man who had come after them, the apes appealed sometimes to a Higher Divinity for success in projects about to be undertaken. Superstition, Religion and Faith was the theological end for all living creatures. Or so it would seem.

"O God," the minister intoned unctuously, "we pray you, bless our Great Army and its Supreme Commander on the eve of a Holy War undertaken for Your sake . . ."

Zaius' face was implacable. Ursus' was smugly superior.

". . . and grant," the minister droned on, "in the name of Your Prophet, our great Lawgiver—" here he genuflected before the statue, his scarlet robes flashing, "that we, Your chosen servants, created and born in Your divine image, may aspire the more perfectly to that spiritual godliness and bodily beauty which You, in Your infinite mercy, have thought fit to deny to our brutal enemies." The impressive words soared.

His bow deepened, his arms described a wide parabola of intense exhortation. The kneeling hierarchy *amened* in low voices.

"So be it," General Ursus murmured mockingly, loud enough for Dr. Zaius to hear.

The statue of the Lawgiver smiled down on everybody.

Brent lay on the nightmarish subway platform, Nova curled up on a broken bench nearby like some immense kitten at sleep. Brent was waking up, after having fallen into a pitifully disturbed slumber alive with ghosts, demons and weird apparitions of his fancy. Blinking his eyes open, he almost groaned aloud at the eerie spectacle that was still before him, surrounding his reason; the mad vision of which he was still an integral part.

The subway station, incrusted with its silent armies of stalactites and stalagmites, continued its *drip, drip, drip*. A haunting, maddening refrain. Wearily, Brent stood up and stretched his stiff, aching limbs. Dazed, he staggered to the sleek wet wall and cupped his hands to catch some of the falling water which ran down steadily from the enormous stalactite overhead. He drank. The water was fresh and cold. It felt good against his parched, sun-baked mouth. He let it dribble down his chin.

He watched the sleeping Nova, his mind tumbling again with imponderables, impossibilities and wild suppositions. He really didn't know what to think. It was all so—so—*incredible*.

"Are *you*," he asked the sleeping girl, "what *we* were before we learned to talk and made fools of ourselves? Did any good ever come of talking—round all those tables? Did apes make war when they were still dumb? Did men?"

Defeatedly, with of course no answer from the girl, he went over to a rocky vent in the station wall, through which some daylight feebly filtered, to look at the outside world from which he and Nova had escaped. He craned his neck to peer through.

He caught his breath, almost jumping back in terror.

About ten yards beyond the vent, he could see a veritable squad of gorilla guards, helmeted, armed, scouring the rocky maze, still obviously searching for him and the girl. He could make out the muttered concert of their ape voices. They didn't sound very happy about something . . .

"I guess we lost them," one of the fiercest-looking gorillas was growling to the others. "The sergeant says, keep looking. We've been here all night. The sergeant says we'd better not come back unless we've found them. Keep looking!"

Brent retreated from the vent, not wanting to see or hear any more. It was still unnerving seeing and hearing animals act like men. The same inflections, the same gestures . . .

He returned to Nova, bent over her, and gently roused her from sleep. She stirred fitfully, her long, curved body tensing.

"Nova, wake up!" he begged.

Instantly she opened her eyes and swung erect. He could see the rapid rise and fall of her semibared breasts within the ragged confines of her burlap-like garments. Her eyes searched his face. He forced a smile.

"We've got to keep moving," he suggested. She nodded, her lips moistening nervously. He took her hand and swung her to her feet. He held onto her hand as he led her carefully down the long, dim, glistening subway platform with its mocking signs and depressing interior that spoke so eloquently of what had happened here many centuries before.

Suddenly he was aware of a faint humming sound.

Hummmmmmmmmmmmmmmmmmmmmmmmmmmm . . .

He reacted. The girl did too.

He hadn't been quite sure he hadn't been hearing things but the awareness on Nova's face was unmistakable.

"That hum. You hear it too!" He exulted, not knowing why. "We're going to follow it . . ."

They did.

All along the platform, using the labyrinth of decayed track and seemingly endless tunnel as a guide. The hum grew gradually louder, with variations of volume and power so subtle that its tone didn't increase abruptly. It merely increased, amplified as it were, to become a steady focus of attention. Excited, Brent clung to the girl, bringing her along behind him. The rhythmic hum and purr of the sound drew him on like a magnet. The tunnel seemed to lengthen, widen, and soon there was no more sign of the platform, the stalactites and stalagmites. None of the rotting, eroded fissures and cracks. The mouth of the cave ahead had rounded out, smoothened. Brent felt as if the way now led upward, that they would eventually surface somewhere in broad daylight in the outer world. But it was only illusion. The underground humming throbbed eerily, built symphonically, and now there was even a faint suggestion of a pleasant wind at their backs, wafting them onward, as if they were two vagrant feathers. It was totally unreal. With his ears filled with the vibrant hum of the unidentifiable noise, with all his senses riveted to an unknown force, Brent walked steadily forward, conscious only of movement and sound.

A long, slightly uphill passage loomed ahead of them.

Glimmering there, somewhere, was a high sliver of very dim light. Indirect light. The hum and the wind had both increased in velocity. They seemed to be hurled forward. Upward. The sliver of light was widening and even as they plummeted toward it, Brent could make out a rock-lined egress of some kind.

The exit was just broad enough to accommodate both of them. Brent's hair floated like a thatch on his head. Nova's long tresses blew like pennants in the breeze. The hum had increased to dynamo intensity. It seemed to fill what was left of this world. The world of the desolate subway station had disappeared entirely.

Before them lay a high-vaulted, natural rock tunnel. With sleek, scaled, impossibly sheer sides. The light source proved to be another vent, set in the rock barrier across the uphill road's dead end ten feet above the ground. Into it seemed to blow—or was it *sucked*, Brent thought wildly—the wind. From this issued the light. Too white to be the sky's and yet . . .

"Whoever—or whatever—is guiding us to this place—" Brent muttered to the girl, "they breathe air, anyway."

They drifted closer to the vent. Two black silhouettes starkly outlined against the bright, white light. The hum, like ten dynamos now, pulsated deafeningly.

Brent and Nova swept closer to the opening, to the weird vent with the weirder light.

He could see it was an octagonal frame, wrought in a white metal of some kind. He stared up at it speculatively, watching the wind rush through the opening. Grimly he got hold of himself. He began to climb toward the vent, putting his hand on the lowest bar of the metallic octagon to do so. Then a frightening thing happened. The electrical hum stopped, as quickly as if he had pushed a contact button. The sudden silence was terrifying.

Brent and the girl stood stock-still, stunned by the new quiet, the strange calm. Nova began to retreat, panicking.

"No," Brent caught her. "It's too late." He drew her back again. "We've got to go on."

But she pulled her hand free of his, shocked by the unknown. Rendered horrified by things she couldn't understand. Brent tried to appeal to her, ignoring that she couldn't follow his words.

"There's a high intelligence at work in this place. Good or bad. That sound we heard is either a warning, or some kind of directional device. I don't know which. But it doesn't matter. The truth is—*they know we're here!*"

She didn't understand a word of it, of course, but his tone was so positive and reassuring that she almost smiled. But she continued to retreat, backing away slowly.

"All right," Brent said. "I'll go up first."

And Brent continued his climb, while Nova watched anxiously. He hauled himself high enough up to grip the octagonal frame. He swung himself in, lost from view for a full second. Nova whimpered aloud. But his head reappeared, silhouetted against the vent. He beckoned. "Don't be afraid. It's empty. Come on."

She reached up to him, climbing. He caught her hand and lifted her. He was very strong. Within seconds, he had swept her up from the strange world of the white tunnel, into the vent, and then they were both suddenly——standing in yet another maze of unreality. On the white floor of a white-walled, down-sloping tunnel, also octagonal in contour. The released air was funneling out of this down toward another white dot of far-off illumination. Another light of some kind. Brent did not hesitate. Pulling Nova, he led her toward the next outlet. The last exit to . . .

Where?

They emerged from the tunnel.

The glaring world of a new daylight invaded their aching eyes.

A cold, unreal sunlight.

And Brent stared.

And Nova shuddered against him. Helpless and afraid again.

For Brent, the universe had once more turned over. His intellect dissolved into a thousand more little pieces.

They were on the outskirts of a city.

City.

If he could have imagined a place that a conceivable nuclear war in the year, say, 1990 might have devastated and then become a refuge of survivors trying to evade fallout, this would be that place. How else to account for the parts of a 2000-year-old original structure that now greeted his eyes? His and the girl's.

He saw twentieth-century brick, stone and concrete, corroded sewer signs, showing through the basic foundations of a metropolis of predominantly white architecture, and the interior decor of a twenty-second-century catacomb complex scooped out of ancient foundations. Narrow streets, more like white corridors, twisted and turned between buildings with windowless walls. There was an unearthly emptiness and nakedness, a lack of ornamentation and color. It was as if a world of impersonal stone greeted them.

"Are we in a city?" Brent whispered. "Or a cemetery?"

Nova stared at him, taking her eyes away from the dead metropolis. She still couldn't understand his words but she had become very sensitive to his moods and emotions. Fear had made them companions.

Wordlessly she slipped her hand into his.

Brent couldn't take his eyes away from the dead city.

It was a stone monster out of his wildest nightmares.

At the Research Complex in Ape City, the scarlet-clad minister had lingered to listen to a heated discussion between Minister of Science Dr. Zaius and General of the Armies Ursus. Though the minister was also an orangutan, it was very clear where his sentiments lay. Zaius felt as though he was boxed in by enemies.

"Supposing they turn out to be our superiors?" Zaius was reinforcing his point.

General Ursus unrolled a map, his expression pugnacious.

"Their territory is no larger than ours. We shall not be outnumbered."

"I was not referring to their numbers," Zaius said patiently. "My supposition concerned their intelligence."

Ursus stared at him, his gimlet eyes cold.

"Then your supposition was blasphemous, Dr. Zaius."

The minister nodded grandly, solemnly agreeing.

"The Lawgiver has written in the Sacred Scrolls that God created Apes in His own image to be Masters of the Earth. We are His Chosen," he reminded Dr. Zaius.

Ursus glowered at the doctor.

"Do you doubt that?" Ursus snapped.

"What I doubt," Zaius said softly, deftly parrying, "is your interpretation of God's intention. Has He ordained that we should make war?"

Ursus rose, pointing with the partly unrolled map.

"Has He ordained that we should die of starvation?"

The minister chimed in again. "Has He ordained that we should make peace with the Human race?"

Zaius brushed that aside. "They are mere animals." It is Zaius who says this.

Ursus snorted, stabbing at the map with a black forefinger. "And these?"

"They are unknown," Zaius said.

"A godly Ape," the minister said unctuously, "is not afraid of the unknown."

"I," said Zaius icily, "am not afraid. I am circumspect."

Ursus jeered slightly, assuming an air of politic joviality, but Zaius was not fooled; there were still those gimlet eyes.

"Still not too circumspect to ride with me on the Day?"

Dr. Zaius seemed to consider that very carefully.

"No." He too rose to his feet. "As a scientist I am also curious."

Zira and Cornelius had worked far into the night on their human guinea pigs. Cornelius took copious notes while his wife ambitiously strove to make one of the caged subhumans learn the power of speech. Zira had worked long and hard on one particularly clever human, making lip gestures and sounds through the bar of the cage. The male human had mimicked her lip movements, heroically.

"*Ma-ma-ma-ma—*" Zira tried and tried again.

The human had tried—but no sounds came forth.

In frustrated fury, Zira had finally given up, turning away in disappointment.

"Oh, Cornelius," she whimpered. "If I could teach *one* of them to talk . . .

Cornelius nodded sympathetically.

She had set herself an impossible task to perform.

Teaching a human *anything* was *never* easy.

8   SPECTERS

There was a stone fountain in the center of the incredible graveyard-city. Brent did not notice it until, magically, it began to spout water. A steady, spurting stream which suddenly and gracefully began to spiral before his eyes. The tiny rippling sounds it made drew him and the girl like a magnet. In the harsh glare of the white stone city with its atmosphere of total antiseptic reality, they both began to drink. Nova lapped at the fluid greedily, like a thirsty dog. Brent drank more slowly, finally straightening when he was sated. Nova continued to drink. Brent watched her.

And then . . .

Abruptly, methodically, with no conscious thought of the movement, he reached down, placed both hands around Nova's neck and forced her head beneath the surface of the pool surrounding the stone fountain.

Nova jerked spasmodically, her entire length stiffening. Brent tightened the grip of his hands, digging into the soft flesh of the girl's neck. He pressed down, mercilessly.

The water rippled, coalesced, shimmered, shattered and rippled into a million extensions of unreality.

Brent increased his hold. Nova spluttered, fighting. Trying to fight back. Drowning . . .

Through a dim haze, Brent saw his own reflection in the agitated waters. Two reflections, really.

The one reflected in the waters of the fountain was an insane parody of his own face. A mask, depicting some intense struggle of mental combat between some outer and inner force over which he had no conscious control. He continued to hold the girl's head below the surface of the fountain pool.

His other face mocked back at him.

Full of pity, horror and astonishment.

The reflected other face was distorted into the visage of some strange monster. A demented, rabid animal with bared teeth and glaring eyes.

Brent's mentality rocked into chaos.

The outer force was saying: *Put my hands around*

her throat. Hold her head down in the water till she dies.

The inner force was fighting back with: *Take my hands off her throat. Get out of my head!*

Brent groaned, mingling a gasp and a grunt, as both forces locked for possession of his soul.

With his hands still clasped about the girl's neck, Brent's voice tore savagely from his throat.

"Take . . . put my hands off . . . round her *throat* . . . hold her . . . *throat* . . . get out of my head . . . down in the water . . . till she . . ." his voice rose in a roar of sound, "DIES!" And then, "No . . . ! NO!"

He wrenched his hands from her throat with a Herculean effort, reeling away from her. For a terrible moment he swayed on his feet, dumbly staring. He felt an appalled sense of horror. Nova came up from the pool, splashing, choking, gagging. She sagged against the stone circular side of the fountain, goggling at him with mingled terror and amazement. Brent fought himself not to approach her. The war in his mind was still raging. *Kill her. Don't kill her.* He shook his head like a confused dog, fighting the outer pressures that wanted to push him toward her, destruction-bound. But Nova remained motionless, mutely staring at him.

Brent's lips barely moved.

"Nova, keep away from her *throat* . . . her bare *throat* in the water until you get *out* . . ." His hand came up in a wild wave. As if pushing something away from himself. He stopped up his ears with both hands. "Get out!" he raged at the silence all around them. "GET OUT OF MY HEAD!"

He backed away from the girl frantically.

She stared up at him, her mouth hanging open.

He pushed out with both hands again.

The fountain—and Nova—receded . . .

Suddenly, his shoulders had touched something.

Huge double doors, abruptly behind him, loomed large and mysterious. Oddly unlocked. Brent's athletic figure swung the doors open. He forced himself back, over a dim threshold, glad of anything that would keep him from harming the girl. Nova grew smaller in his erratic vision. He stopped, only for a second, to call back to her. For she was taking a hesitant step toward him, slender arms outspread.

"Wait for me—" Brent whispered, still fighting the forces engulfing him. "Nova—!" His brain was on fire. Her figure wavered in his sight. Shouting hysterically, Brent crossed the dark threshold and slammed the double doors behind him to close out the horror in his head. To block off Nova from his violence.

She disappeared from view.

Brent hung exhausted against the curved metal door grips on the inside and fought to catch his breath. For a long moment he wrestled with his inner and outer wills. Then he quietened. The strange fit had momentarily passed. He sucked air into his lungs and shuddered. Then he pulled himself erect once more. Turning, he surveyed the interior of this building he had fled into as a sanctuary from insanity.

The unrealities again ruled.

Even here.

He was in a cathedral.

In direct contrast to the bright white glare without, here was only blessed gloom. Brent's eyes roved quickly.

He saw a row of wooden pews flanking a great arched nave. There was a threshold up front, past the choir stalls, beyond the pews. He saw a *prie-dieu* directly below a high altar of some kind. Brent blinked in the occult semidarkness.

There was a *man* standing on the sacred threshold up front.

A white-robed, white-hooded apparition, kneeling in

homage or religious fealty of some kind. A figure as
still as any statue. The figure had not moved when the
great doors had slammed shut. Brent, for all his dazed
condition, recognized in that tiny unimportant fact a
universal truth and oddity: *why shouldn't a cathedral
door always be open to devotees?*

Brent watched the hooded figure, not daring to
breathe. Or even speak. The hush of the place was
emotionally demoralizing.

The hood lifted upward, the robed arms spread out
like bat wings and a sonorous voice suddenly intoned:
"*I reveal my Inmost Self unto my God!*" The voice
rang with the clarity and persuasion of unshakable
faith and belief. Brent found his eyes ranging upward,
following the direction of the stentorian declaration.

Slowly, from the space of darkness above the high
altar, an eerie light appeared. Growing, expanding, as
if on a rheostat; the gloom transformed from dim illumination to a full, blazing intensity. The outflung arms
of the hooded figure held in a posture of crucifixion.
And utter adoration.

Brent saw what the new light held.

Not a statue of Christ.

Not even some strange unknown pagan god.

The hooded figure's exhortations were for something else.

The ultimate blasphemy.

Something mounted and enthroned and positioned
with all the care and reverence of any highly esteemed
religious curio.

A Twentieth-Century Atom Bomb.

Perfectly preserved and slung, like some great inverted cross, between two supporting brackets of
hammered gold, it hung from the arched nave in all its
illuminated wonder. On one of its impressive steel fins
there were stenciled the two Greek letters: *ALPHA*
and *OMEGA*.

The Beginning and the End.

Brent stared in mounting horror from the depths of the double doors. *"In a church——?"* His racked whisper was alien to his own ears. It was as if someone else had spoken.

A tiny scratch of sound came on the door behind him. Back to the barrier, Brent suddenly drew taut. The scratching continued. He closed his eyes. *"Nova?"* The scratching burbled into a flurry of sounds. Brent slid both hands into the door grips, blocking the portals with his body, his muscles congealing into lead. He didn't budge. "Keep away, Nova," he whispered urgently to the door. "Keep away from me—and from here . . ."

But the tapping had become almost a crescendo, punctuated with fist-pounding and low moans of appeal. Brent tightened his resolve; perspiration broke out on his forehead. He couldn't let the girl in here, no matter what happened . . .

The hooded figure on the dais had turned.

An ornate panel at his side, with three jeweled buttons of emerald, topaz and ruby set into the top of the *prie-dieu*, was pressed. Brent saw the gesture, realizing that the figure had heard Nova's attempts to get in.

The figure rose to its full height and made another gesture. Brent started. He knew somehow, with some weird sense of comprehension, that what he was seeing was the *Sign of the Bomb*.

An inverted Sign of the Cross. With the figure making a vertical downward gesture to depict the body of the Bomb and then two lateral gestures to indicate the fins at its base. The supreme sacrilege! A sign from Hell.

The whole cathedral suddenly flooded with new light.

Even as Nova continued to pound away, the hooded figure came down from the dais and stalked toward

Brent huddled at the doors of the strange place of worship. And when the pounding stopped, with Brent blinking in the sudden fresh glare of illumination, the hooded figure advanced like a specter. Brent wondered at the silence beyond the door. He started to open it, then checked himself and turned to confront the advancing figure. Nova was forgotten.

The hood framed a face of startling purity.

The man drew closer and halted, staring at Brent. Brent stared back.

He assumed that the man was the verger of this strange cathedral. But beyond that, the appearance of the face before him was astounding.

The man was tall, of an indecipherable age, but his face was one of great beauty. Unwrinkled skin, as smooth as marble, deep-set luminous eyes in shadowed sockets, with the barest accentuation of lip line, which somehow makes a man or a woman look sexy. The man's mouth seemed to speak. To say something. But Brent heard nothing, *orally*.

"What did you say?" Brent asked fiercely, frightened again.

The verger had said *nothing*.

He merely stood there, regarding Brent.

"What do you mean, there's no point?" Brent answered the unspoken words he heard in his own brain. "Will they hurt her?"

Again the verger's lips did not move.

"Maybe not physically," Brent agreed. "But you can hurt *here*." He tapped his own head. "I know."

The verger spoke his unheard words.

"Yes, it's gone now," Brent answered. "But outside—" Suddenly he twitched. A great spasm took hold of him. His eyes leaped. "Your lips don't move. Your lips don't move . . . but I can hear . . . no, not *hear* —I mean I *know* what you are thinking."

The fixed grin left the verger's face.

Brent nodded. "I saw nothing. You were in darkness."

The verger spoke again, silently.

Brent looked quickly over his shoulder. His mind raced to remain calm, to keep pace with this new-found unreality.

Two men had appeared at the double doors behind him. Unarmed, but strangely alien and enigmatically marble-faced; two more denizens of this strange and terrible city. They touched Brent's elbows briefly with the fingertips of velvet-textured hands.

"All right, all right," he muttered, not resisting.

Unable to understand, incapable of assessing anything, he allowed himself to be led out of the cathedral. The verger remained where he was. Shadowy, inscrutable. But now there was a worried gleam in the deep-set luminous eyes.

There was no sign of Nova beyond the big doors.

But around the stone fountain, capering in the awful white glare of the city's atmosphere, were a dozen or more children of many races and ages. Their squeals of pleasure sounded grotesque in the daylight. Brent restrained a shudder. The children had ringed the fountain, romping in a dancing circle, their voices gaily blending in a terrible refrain:

> Ring-a-ring o'neutrons
> A pocketful of positrons
> A fission! A fission!
> We all fall down!

On the last word, they spilled backward, forming a star shape, and lay deathly still. Like some dreadful parody of an old Busby Berkeley musical dance routine from one of the old Warner Brothers movies of the thirties. Brent shuddered again, remembering—it was only a game, wasn't it? But . . .

The silent guards egged him on, courteously almost,

gently prodding his elbows again. Brent kept on moving. The playing children were soon lost somewhere behind him. The ghastly white complex of the metropolis engaged all of his attention. The tomblike buildings jutting sheer from the barren earth. The all-encompassing glare of white and cold daylight. Dimly he could hear the echoing words of the playing children as they picked up yet another chorus of the deadly song. It sounded like something they had learned by rote. A Child's Garden of Verses set to the meaning and reality of a terrible code of destruction and doom. Armageddon set to Mother Goose!

It was terrifying.

And he had no idea where Nova was. Or what they might have done to her. Whoever *They* were.

They!

In his torn-apart and beleaguered intellect, he was no longer able to make any judgments or solve any mental problems. His entire universe of consciousness and stable thinking was awry; he had lost all sense of rhythm, balance and common sense.

He was only hurtingly aware of one great truth.

He had fled from the mockery of the Great Apes into something perhaps twice as alien, a dozen times more hazardous. A hopeless morass of terror, horror and who knew what else?

Meaning—he had jumped from the frying pan directly into the fire.

As perhaps—Taylor had?

It was too early to tell. Too early to tell anything.

He didn't know.

He might never know.

Blindly, obediently, he suffered himself to be led by the marble-faced guards to another part of this Crazy House forest.

All he did wish, and hope for, with every fiber of

whatever of his being still belonged to him by right
of his own individuality, was that the girl was all right.

Safe.

Unharmed.

Untouched by the madness that seemed to surround
him on all sides. The sheer glare of lunacy that had
become a part of all his waking reflexes and responses.
And reactions.

Not even H. G. Wells at his wildest, not even Jules
Verne, had dared conceive of a civilization dedicated
to the Bomb.

This, indeed, was a journey into the Absurd.

And the terribly frightening——

*For he knew that he was somewhere on Fifth Ave-
nue and the vaulted building he had just left was St.
Patrick's Cathedral!*

9   MENDEZ

Another white corridor.

Another trip into isolation and weird world-within-
worlds.

Brent, flanked by his grim guards, found himself
being ushered down a long bare corridor, a narrow
passageway which was lined all along the route with
uniform busts, honoring some form of dynastic suc-
cession. It wasn't until the last bleak, awesome stone
head and shoulders that Brent got any inkling of what
he was seeing. This last impressively mounted face had
a plaque at its base which proclaimed in etched letter-

ing: MENDEZ XXVI. Mendez the Twenty-Sixth!
Brent wagged his head, to clear it of cobwebs.

At last the guards led him through another door.
Into another room.

And another nightmare. In broad daylight.

It was a room shaped like an amphitheater, with
curved white walls, the hallway forming a well below.
This was where Brent and the two guards stood, waiting for some kind of audience. At the head of the
room, Brent could see the living replica of that last bust
in the narrow passageway. The same smooth marble
face, the luminous eyes, the glasslike rigidity. All of it
enveloped in brilliant purple robes, lying like a shroud
about the imposing figure of Mendez the Twenty-
Sixth, as he sat like a judge presiding in some Supreme
Court conclave of this incredible city. Brent stared up
at the paradox of five robed inquisitor-rulers, sitting in
carved chairs, regarding him with an impassivity of
gaze that was bloodcurdling in its lack of human emotion. Brent held his ground, staring back. His eyes,
which had been the most important part of his physical
tools these last terrible hours, were now fully strung to
the maximal pitch of their efficiency. Seeing was believing—but here, in this awful new world, it was also dis-
believing. The senses, all five of them, could assimilate
only so much.

His eyes swept over Mendez and his court.

He saw a magnificent Negro, robed all in white, his
onyx face startling in contrast with his garments. He
saw a mountainous fat man, serene and cool, garbed
in red robes. To Mendez's left, there was a woman—
a strikingly beautiful woman, whose ivory face rose
like an orchid from a gown of sheer blue. To Mendez's
right, a green-robed elder-statesman type—very much
like the mysterious verger—squatted prominently. But
unlike his companions, this one was almost charming

and cheerful in demeanor. Brent was reminded of a Puck, grown to ancient years.

All five of these phantasmagorical figures struck Brent like some odd concatenation of Rembrandt's famous *Syndics of the Cloth Guild*. With the terrible difference of an imposed horror. And the fantasy of the Unknown.

He waited, wondering, trying to control the fear moving like a snake in his stomach.

He didn't realize that the five seated figures, looking down, could see him directly. Or that if they looked straight ahead, they could see, projected on the opposite wall, the visual impress of their own thought projections. Brent had no way of knowing into what technological wonderworld he had stumbled, though his encounter with the verger had given him some advance notice of the miracles to be found in this strange city.

Each "wall image" was projected in color to identify the sender. Thus, white for the Negro, blue for the beautiful girl, red for the fat man, green for the puckish statesman type. And purple for Mendez himself. This Brent was yet to learn, for he could not see the wall behind him.

Nor could he yet fully understand the traumatic hypnosis that the people of this civilization could inflict upon him. As they had done with him at the water fountain in that episode with Nova. Brent's own stubbornness would bring on such an attack.

The practitioner merely had to close his eyes, project to the wall in his own color scheme, and Brent would remain in pain and agony until the particular inquisitor opened his eyes.

This was the mad world into which Brent had all unknowingly stumbled. The phenomenon of A.D. 3955!

Brent felt himself the target of Mendez, the Negro, the woman, the fat man and the elder statesman.

He knew they were talking to him; he *felt* it even though he could hear no words, see no lips move, and knew nothing about the wall behind him with its color-scheme code of interrogation.

Mendez said nothing.

The fat man jerked his head ever so slightly.

The far wall lit up in red colors.

"Brent," Brent answered.

The fat man jerked his head again.

"John Christopher," Brent said politely. "And who are *you?*"

Another jerk.

"I see—" Brent found himself understanding, in spite of the impossibility of it all. And the improbability. "You—are the only reality in the universe. Everything else is illusion. Well, that's nice to know."

The red colors flared on the opposite wall. The others said nothing.

"I got here by accident," Brent explained to the fat man. "How did *you* get here?"

There was no answer from the fat man.

As the interview progressed, a pattern began to become very clear. The fat man probed for facts, the woman for emotional feelings, the elder statesman for beliefs and opinions. The Negro would ask no questions at all. He was there merely to induce pain; the catalyst for the workings of man's conscience. Brent only sensed all this. He could not have said where the knowledge came from.

Mendez sat through it all, implacable as a Buddha.

The elder statesman now jerked his head, his genial smile almost benevolent. But only *almost*.

It was like being caught in a cross-fire of four machine guns. Only you could not hear the whine and twang of bullets. Only the ferocity of the assault hit you like some withering invisible hail of terror.

Openmouthed, Brent once more answered.

"You're way off. Why should I want to *spy* on you? Personally, I'm not even sure you exist." It was true. Was it all a bad dream? Would he awaken on the reconnaissance spacecraft to find Skipper poking him to get up?

The puckish inquisitor jerked his head.

"Certainly I know who I am," Brent rasped impatiently. "I'm an astronaut. I'm here because I'm lost."

No surprise showed on the five faces up above him. Only a sudden interest. Mendez's eyes glistened like a cat's.

The fat man again jerked his head.

"From this planet," Brent answered him. "But from another time. Two thousand years ago."

There was still no surprise evident. Only that deepening of interest in the marble faces above him.

"I know, it sounds insane. But if so, it's *my* insanity, not yours. So I can abolish you—all of you—anytime I choose."

They all smiled at that. Benevolently. Matching the elder statesman's habitual facade.

Brent bit his lip.

He could not see the opposite wall.

The inquisitors had projected, in their various color schemes, a montage of all that had happened.

An image of Taylor, looking like some prehistoric Tarzan, with a bedraggled Nova-Eve in tow, was shown approaching buried New York. The last shot left him striking the wall of ice and vanishing into its wilderness, with Nova screaming behind him.

"No, I don't know how to get back," Brent almost mumbled, still oblivious of the story on the wall. "We came through a defect—a kind of slipping in Time itself."

He caught himself, feeling a wave of self-pity swamping him. "My skipper died. I'm alone."

Instantly, the images of Taylor and the girl on the

wall vanished. They were supplanted by five images of
Nova all by herself, wandering in the desert wilderness.
And then——

She was projected in all of the inquisitorial colors:

The fat man saw her pulling herself through the
octagonal vent. A burst of flaming red.

The beautiful woman saw her asleep in Brent's arms
on the bench in the public square. A shimmering blue
ocean of color.

Mendez saw her hammering on the outside of the
cathedral's double door. A purple flash of violence.

The elder statesman envisioned her being seized and
removed by the guards on duty in the strange city. A
twisting garland of green.

Only the Negro's wall remained colorless. Bare,
blank and white.

The beautiful woman in blue jerked her lovely face.

Brent was instantly on the defensive.

"Who?" he hesitated.

The woman jerked again.

"Nova?" Brent lied. "What's that? A star? A gal-
axy?" His heart pounded with sudden alarm for the
girl.

At that, the Negro shut his eyes.

Brent cried out. A poker-hot inferno ignited his
skull. His brain revolved in stunning flashes of agony.
He went down to his knees, tears coming to his eyes.
The Negro opened his eyes. Slowly.

Gradually, painfully, Brent straightened. The agony
had left as suddenly as it had come.

"I know her—yes . . ."

Silence greeted that.

Brent lost his temper, shouting, "She's harmless! Let
her alone!"

The Negro closed his eyes again.

Rivets of white-hot pain hit Brent from every direction. He went down again, writhing as his entire body

was stitched and needled with agonizing pinpricks. He clutched his stomach as if he had been poisoned. His vitals were on fire. His face twisted, his tongue lolled. "All right—" the breath forced itself from his lungs. "I'll—tell you!"

Smiling, the Negro opened his beautiful eyes.

The woman jerked her head again.

"I didn't find her," Brent gasped. "She found me."

Again, a jerk.

"Two days ago."

Another jerk.

"Don't be crude," Brent groaned. "I'm fond of her. And grateful . . ."

The beautiful woman arched her head once more.

"Because she helped me!"

Another tilt of that lovely face.

"To break out of Ape City."

All five of the faces looming over him leaned forward. Now all of the heads twitched in unison. Brent's hands shot to his ears. They were engulfing him from all sides, attacking on every front of his personality and intelligence.

"Stop!" he begged. "I can't understand——can't separate——you're all screaming at me—at the same time! Please . . ."

He groveled, still blocking his ears in order to hear nothing more. Suddenly, incredibly, the face of Mendez softened. His rubbery lips parted and a deep, mellifluous voice sounded in the chamber of new horrors. Brent stared up at him in amazement.

"He's right," Mendez said. "He has only limited intelligence. We should speak aloud. And one at a time. Albina." He looked at the strikingly beautiful woman in blue.

The woman stared down at Brent, her impeccable face almost kind and sympathetic. But it was the illusion of her beauty and her rich, deep tones.

"Are we to apprehend," she said, soothingly, "that you—were in the City of the Apes . . . ?"

Brent, tremendously gratified though nothing had changed, nodded eagerly. The chamber didn't seem so terrifying any more.

"Yes. Two days ago."

The fat man intervened. "What did you see?"

Brent dodged that, side-stepping the question. "You're talking . . ."

The elder statesman nodded cheerfully. "Certainly, we can all talk. A rather primitive accomplishment. We use it when we have to. I, Caspay, consider it a vulgar thing."

"When we pray," the fat man interjected again.

"When we sing to God," the Negro said fervently.

Then all of them, all five on the dais, made the hateful Sign of the Bomb. Brent winced, in memory of that sleek monster atop the high altar of the cathedral. *St. Patrick's—my God!*

"Your God—what a joke! You worship something we made two thousand years ago. An atom bomb!"

The fat man heaved a long and ponderous sigh. The folds of his fat stomach wriggled beneath his red robes.

"Ah. You've seen the Bomb, Mr. Brent."

"Above the altar in your cathedral. An obscenity . . ."

All the inquisitors rose as one in response to his heated indignation. Their faces were ominous. Even Caspay was no longer smiling. Regal Mendez rose like a lean colossus, his eyes flashing.

"Mr. Brent, you have beheld God's instrument on Earth!" he intoned majestically. He motioned his fellow inquisitors to be seated. He alone remained standing.

He looked down at Brent.

"For it is written that, in the First Year of the Bomb

—the blessing of the Holy Fallout descended from above . . ."

"What kind of nonsense is that?" Brent interrupted harshly. Mendez ignored him.

". . . and my people built a new city in the blackened bowels of the old . . ."

"Nonsense!" Brent roared, trembling, angry.

"Blessed be the Bomb Everlasting—" Mendez droned on.

"Utter nonsense . . ."

". . . to whom alone we may reveal our inmost truth, and whom we shall serve all our days in peace."

"Until you fire it at the apes," Brent concluded sarcastically.

There was fresh silence at that. Mendez then stirred. His deep eyes held strange lights in them.

"You don't understand." With a rustle of his purple robes, he sat down again. "The Bomb is a Holy Weapon of Peace."

Brent began to laugh.

He couldn't help it.

Amusement shook him. A terrible humor that put aside all concern for his own safety. The Negro shut his eyes. Quickly. Sadly almost.

More pain, more mental injections of torture, made Brent a writhing, twisting, burlesque of a human being on the floor of the chamber. Animal sounds tore from his throat. He sounded half bestial.

The Negro waited a full minute and then reopened his eyes.

"We're a patient people, Mr. Brent," he said softly, his voice nevertheless filling the chamber. "We can repeat this little lesson as often as we want. Because we are determined to know what the apes want. War, or peace."

Brent waited for the waves of agony and nausea to recede. He recovered more slowly this time. He propped himself up on his hands and knees, fighting off hysteria. Caspay's puckish voice came down to him, reprovingly.

"Try to understand—the only weapons we have are purely illusion."

Albina's soothing contralto filtered down too.

"You *imagined* he was hurting you."

Brent smiled at her crookedly, shaking his head.

"Because *I* imagined I was hurting you," the Negro explained without malice. "Are you in pain now?"

"No," Brent admitted.

"No *imaginary* bones broken? Or blood flowing?" The Negro's voice took on echoes of sadism; he was enjoying his thoughts. "Or eyeballs bursting? Or guts spilling?"

"No," Brent said, louder than before.

"Then I have *hurt* but not *harmed* you," the Negro affirmed.

Albina smiled triumphantly.

"Traumatic Hypnosis is a weapon of peace."

Caspay's eyes twinkled mysteriously.

"Like the Visual Deterrent."

Before Brent had time to ask what that was, there was a mammoth *whooosh* of sound and within a yard of where he stood, a pillar of flame shot up. Brent reeled back. A vertical geyser jet of steam behind him licked at his rear so that he had to stumble forward again. Only to be cut off by the wall of fire. Between two horrors.

"Or the Sonic Deterrent," Caspay chuckled delightedly.

Abruptly there was a *rat-tat-tat*, a gobbling medley of rapid-fire noises to the right of where Brent stood imprisoned. As if an invisible machine gun had cut loose. Then to his left, an ear-skewering electronic scream of sound rose in such deafening volume that soon the entire chamber and the outside world seemed to reverberate with the caterwauling. The sounds rose to a deafening tumult, then just when Brent was sure his eardrums would explode, vanished with terrifying, miraculous abruptness. His body swayed with the assault from all sides.

"Weapons," Caspay continued blandly, "of peace, Mr. Brent."

"Like all our weapons," the beautiful Albina agreed from her sea of blue robes.

The Negro nodded firmly. "Mere illusion."

Brent lost his temper and what was left of his discretion. He had been a toy for too long; a mere mortal buffeted and battered about by what was seemingly an impossible manifest destiny.

"Damn your hypocrisy!" he bellowed.

The Negro turned to look at Caspay. Then he looked at his white wall. There, projected, was an image of Brent set afire, clothes and flesh blazing, screaming soundlessly in a void of death. Caspay returned his gaze down to Brent. His expression was gentle.

"We very much need your help, Mr. Brent."

"Why?" It was a helpless groan from Brent.

"We are the Keepers of the Divine Bomb. That is our only reason for survival. And yet—as you see—we are defenseless."

Brent sneered. Bitterly.

"Yes, I can see that."

"Defenseless," Caspay continued, "against the monstrous, slobbering, materialistic apes."

"I'll help nobody!" Brent rallied, with deep but slow confusion. "I hope you annihilate one another."

Caspay smiled.

"Mr. Brent, I apologize for your language. There are times, I know, when your sanity—is about to give way. I hope that doesn't happen. I hope you can tell us . . ."

"Exactly," the fat man interrupted again, as seemed

to be his conversational forte, "what the apes are planning!"

Brent didn't understand. He couldn't.

Albina stirred anew. Silky, sinister, maddeningly lovely.

"We've caught some of their scouts. Hideous creatures. We had them here—precisely where you're standing. But either their skulls are too thick. Or they actually know *nothing* . . ."

"And neither do I," Brent cut her off violently. "And if I did, I wouldn't tell you."

The Negro laughed. It was a very unpleasant sound. He gazed at his white wall again.

On it, Nova materialized.

Caspay said gently, "You make me very sad, Mr. Brent."

Brent looked from the Negro to Caspay, frowning. His mind tried to find an answer. And then, amazingly, he saw Nova being brought into the chamber, struggling between another set of implacable guards. The girl was clawing, scratching, but the guards might have been zombis. Nova, despite her torn garments, or perhaps because of them, looked more paganly desirable than ever. Brent bunched his fists, trembling.

"She can't help you," he blurted. "She can't even talk. Don't harm her . . ."

Albina made a low, feline sound in her silky throat and motioned regally to the guards who now released Nova. The girl, crying, ran headlong into Brent's arms. He clasped her to him, reveling in the feel of her once more. He had ached to hold her again, without knowing it. Or realizing why.

"Of course not, Mr. Brent," Albina purred. "We never harm anyone. *You* are going to harm her." Her ivory face pulsed sensually. Her exquisite bosom rose and fell as she breathed deeply.

Smiling sadistically, his great black face wreathed in
onyx power, the Negro closed his eyes. A grim Golem
created for torment, dedicated to the art of cruelty.

Brent went into action like an automaton.

Mendez the Twenty-Sixth, royally purple and ma-
jestic, watched with great attention from his central
position on the dais.

He and his four inquisitors, red, blue, green and
white.

The weird magic of the wall shattered all that was
left of Brent's power to fight back.

The chamber looked down on madness.

10   MASKS

Brent closed in on Nova.

He took her in his arms and unexpectedly kissed her
on the trembling mouth. The Negro kept his eyes
tightly closed. Mendez and the others watched, waiting. Their faces were a study in expectancy. Brent was
oblivious of them. All of his being, his soul and his
mind and body, was centralized on Nova. The girl in
his arms.

The chamber held the odd tableau, like a pin point in
the march of time, freezing the moment for all eternity
itself.

Brent's kiss was tender at first. Then some raging
passion consumed him. Nova, bewildered, rode along
with the first wave of bodily hunger embroiling her
and Brent in this fantastic embrace.

The Negro's eyes remained shut.

The kiss went from the loving to the lustful.

And then from the lustful to the lethal.

For all her unschooled, uncivilized, unsophisticated naivete, Nova sensed the difference. Brent caught her fast in a viselike hold that was all cruelty and mad desire. Nova recoiled in his arms, trying to shake him off, to run, to hide. Brent was remorseless. Now he had her trapped. He was pinching her nostrils, suffocating her mouth with his own. His other hand was digging into her flesh, tearing at her full breasts. He kept on hammering at her, cruelly hurting her until her weak struggles grew even weaker.

And the Negro did not open his eyes.

"Tell us about the apes, Mr. Brent," the fat man said in a loud, clear voice.

The Negro's eyes blinked open.

Brent released Nova, suddenly. She slipped from his grasp to the stone floor, sprawling in a lifeless spill of arms and legs. Brent stared down at her dumbly, appalled.

"Tell us about the apes," the fat man repeated his request.

Brent fought to regain his mind; a compound of bewildered horror and returning intelligence. He knew he had to talk but somehow he also knew he must lie. Anything to save Nova from a possible death *and* the Bomb from potential activation. These people, whatever they were, no matter how intelligent and advanced, were all mad! *Mad!*

Shrilly, he found his voice. Anything to keep the Negro from closing his eyes again.

"The apes are a primitive, semiarticulate and underdeveloped race whose weapons have not progressed beyond the club and the sling!"

"You're lying," the fat man interposed, "and we know it!"

Caspay spoke up. "The ape scouts had rifles, Mr. Brent."

Brent said nothing to that. Wearily, the Negro closed his eyes.

Brent raised a brutal foot above Nova's insensate body. Within him rockets exploded, pain flashed, terrible ideas and thoughts took tangible shapes and forms.

His chest was on fire. Still he struggled against bringing his foot down to smash that lovely, defenseless figure.

"They should fall . . . an easy prey . . ." he gasped, "to *stamp* on the many peaceful weapons at your *dispose* . . . of her with your foot on her belly and *stamp* . . . GET OUT OF MY HEAD!" he snarled at the eyes-shut Negro who loomed above him.

The fat man spoke again when the Negro reopened his eyes.

"Tell us again about the apes, Mr. Brent. The first time—was not quite true, was it?"

"How do you *know*?" Brent raged at him. "How do you *know*?"

Quickly he knelt beside Nova, cradling her head in his hand, his senses all whirling, convoluting, pinwheeling riotously.

From behind the inquisitors, the wall threw up more projections. Taylor again. Taylor stumbling. Taylor heroically lost . . .

Nova, coming to in Brent's arms, saw the wall from her position on the floor. Five images of Taylor, in red, white, blue, green and purple, sliding into identifiable focus. Her eyes widened, her lush mouth tried to form the name, "Tay-lor." Brent could not see or understand her. He was too concerned with the terrible thought that he might have harmed her. Suddenly she lifted a feeble hand, trying to point at the far wall.

Simultaneously, the inquisitors lowered their eyes. The wall images vanished.

Brent saw only the bright white nothingness when his own eyes sought what Nova was seeing.

Caspay smiled ingratiatingly.

"Now—what may we hope for in the way of help?"

"Nothing," Brent muttered. "Unless you set us free. Me—and her."

Caspay's smile hardened subtly.

"You *are* free, Mr. Brent. Free to do what *we* will."

Mendez the Twenty-Sixth made a motion with his hand.

"Now," he commanded.

The fat man said, "Tell us about the apes, Mr. Brent."

Brent took a long pause. He looked at Nova, looked at the council, and then shrugged helplessly.

"The apes are marching on your city," he said quietly.

A great silence descended on the Chamber of Interrogation. The five robed figures digested the information, each to his own intensity. The opposite wall came alive again with varying degrees of color.

Brent hugged Nova to him, glad only of the fact that she was still alive.

That they *both* were.

He could feel her heart beating like a bird's against his chest.

Ape City was aquiver with the sounds of an army in motion. Riding together at the head of long columns of mounted horsemen and rolling gun carriages, were General Ursus and Dr. Zaius. Behind them, the tramp of feet, the pound of horses' hooves and the clatter of arms sounded through the streets and roadways of the settlement. The Grand Army of the Apes was on the march at last. Trooping past the house of Zira and Cornelius, taking the same uphill country route to the Forbidden Zone as had Brent and Nova. Ursus was in his glory. Bemedaled, befitting a military monarch, Ursus was in the full panoply of his being. Zaius, thoughtful and a trifle sardonic, rode at his side, musing to himself on the pomposity and pitfalls of self-imposed delusions of grandeur. He was sure Ursus was riding for a fall. But one, unfortunately, that might take Ape City with it! And all the important work that Zaius and his colleagues had labored for years to bring about.

As they rode by the house of Cornelius and Zira, Zaius dared not hazard a look at their intelligent faces. He knew what the expression on those faces would be. Rueful and scowling!

The Grand Army moved along, clattering, jubilant, eager for an engagement, a test of its skills. General Ursus' horse fairly pranced. The general was all smiles and superiority. Sure of Gorilla Might and Gorilla Power. The pompous idiot!

From the window of their domestic castle, Cornelius and Zira were indeed witnessing the spectacle of Might on the Move.

Zira was disgusted, as always.

"Dr. Zaius is with him. Some people's convictions are about as deep as a mild case of *mange*."

"They have to show unity," Cornelius argued. Not too strongly.

"So should the chimpanzees."

"But, Zira," Cornelius protested. "We're too few. We'd be cutting our own throats. How can *we* take any initiative, while—" he gestured toward the rolling gorilla army trooping past their home, "*they're* here."

They watched as the rear columns of Ursus' forces passed the house and receded up the hill, going away, disappearing into the horizon. Zira snorted, her cute face puckered.

"Has it occurred to you that tomorrow—they *won't* be here?"

Cornelius looked at her.

Their eyes locked.

A patient, knowing smile curled Zira's mouth.

Cornelius swallowed nervously.

It was pretty obvious what his adorable, firm-minded little wife meant. What she had always meant, since the very beginning of unrest.

Revolt!

Miles up the road, moving briskly in broad sunny daylight, the Grand Army was making good time. Ursus, Zaius, a bugler, the vanguard and vanguard commander, had rounded a corner on the outskirts of Ape City, to be confronted by a sight not to Ursus' liking. Or Zaius' for that matter. Being the only non-gorilla in the group, Zaius was keenly affected by the spectacle of a chimpanzee student demonstration.

Half a dozen earnest, outspoken young chimpanzees were squatting directly across the line of march, sitting in the roadway, blocking the advance of the Grand Army of Apes. Ursus growled menacingly in his deep chest. The two demonstrators in the center of the pathetically valiant little group were holding aloft a banner on which the paint-scrawled plea GIVE US PEACE was clearly visible and advisory. Ursus' brow darkened. Zaius feared the worst.

"Halt," Ursus commanded in an undertone to the bugler.

The primitive horn blared a tinny signal which was picked up and relayed by successive buglers all down the column of gorillas and guns. The column came to a full stop some twenty yards from the little knot of demonstrators barring the roadway.

Ursus, almost chidingly, smiled down at the chimpanzees.

"Get off the road, young people."

The "young people" continued to sit, ignoring him and his army, obstinately and sincerely contemptuous of Ursus and all he might do in retaliation. Zaius' eyes narrowed.

Ursus wheeled to the vanguard commander, braking his mount.

"Get them out of the way!" he bellowed.

The commander leered and drew a heavy pistol from his uniformed middle, but Zaius, quickly reaching across, took the ugly muzzle in both his paws.

"Wait," he urged. He turned on General Ursus. Their eyes dueled again. "We don't want martyrs, do we?"

General Ursus said to the commander, "And do it quietly."

The demonstrators had gone limp in the roadway, the usual weapon of advocates of non-violence. The commander rapped out some orders and soon, and swiftly, gorilla hands had lifted the demonstrators, carrying them by the arms and legs and piling them into the cage-wagons at the army's disposal, closing out the incident. The army was able to advance again. Wheels rolled over the abandoned peace signs. Ursus smiled smugly at Dr. Zaius. The good doctor stared pointedly ahead, his eyes on some unseen calamity on the horizon. In the future. With the inscrutability that General Ursus was never able to connect with the seething anger that boiled inside Dr. Zaius' intellectual breast. Something his ape mentality would never have understood. Or *liked*.

Dr. Zaius knew how to wait.

To bide his time.

Without giving up his ideals or his ethics to the code of Brute Force. To the ethos of Ape Logic and Ape Stupidity. *Gorilla*, that is.

General Ursus did not care.

So long as he had things his own way.

He would show the good doctor the efficacy of Power in due time.

All in due time.

Briskly, blindly, unknowingly, Ursus led his marching legions toward the horrors of the Forbidden Zone.

Where he thought the Fist would solve everything.

Where Dr. Zaius knew it would not.

In the great cathedral where the Bomb was lord and master of all it surveyed, a mass was in progress. The vaulted reaches of the dimly lit nave echoed with the chorus of voices raised in adoring harmony to the words of the hymn known as Psalm to Mendez II.

To Brent, forced to attend the weird ritual, the entire schema was a frightening mutation of the ancient Christian observance. All the singing and chanting seemed to have its origins in sacred songs of the twentieth century, now all cannibalized to match the coldness and cruel barrenness of this strange new cosmos into which he had blundered. He wondered how it all must sound to the mute Nova, at his side in the front pew, flanked by the fat man, Caspay, the beauteous Albina and the Negro, with four armed guards directly behind them.

At the high altar, now dark, Mendez stood facing a congregation of white-robed listeners. Brent was struck by the demeanor of the entire gathering. An inward spiritual serenity hovered about every face and figure. An outward gracefulness and gentility in mocking contrast with the *reason* for the radiance and exaltation of those faces and singing voices. The Bomb hung suspended above the altar, still invisible in the gloom of the ceiling.

Mendez was chanting sonorously, his purple robes dazzling as his arms and his voice rose in unison:

"The heavens declare the glory of the Bomb. And the firmament showeth his handiwork."

To a man, woman and child, the congregation answered him. A full-throated, deep, reverent response. The gloomy cathedral echoed with the words:

"*His sound is gone out unto all lands. And His light unto the ends of the world.*"

Now the hidden choir joined with Mendez in an invocation that soared up to the nave. The sound was spectral, ghostly:

"He descended from the outermost part of heaven. And there is nothing hid from the heat thereof. There is neither speech nor language. But His voice is heard among them."

The congregation responded:

"*Praise him. My strength and my redeemer.*"

Mendez knelt at the *prie-dieu;* his white-gloved hand pressed a button on the bejeweled panel. The floodlight control was released and dramatically, illuminatingly, the Great Bomb, with its inscribed fins, filled the eye. ALPHA and OMEGA glowed like constellations in a sky of gun-metal silver.

Mendez and the choir sung aloud:

"Glory be to the Bomb and to the Holy Fallout—As it was in the beginning, is now, and ever shall be; world without end. Amen."

"*Amen,*" the congregation spoke as one.

Brent had a bad taste in his mouth. His ears ached with the awful, ridiculous, puling blasphemy of it all. Behind him, the four guards, their faces radiant and inspired, were singing with brilliant sincerity. The fat man, Caspay, Albina and the Negro were showing nothing of the revulsion that beat through Brent's brain like a prairie fire. Only he and Nova, of all the souls in that damned cathedral, were remote and out of place and out of time. Their rags may have been covered at last with decent robes, but nothing had changed. Brent was still frightened and repulsed by all that he saw and heard.

The multitude of *Amens* fell away to a whisper.

And still the Bomb gleamed down from its religious base. The main lights of the cathedral had all dimmed, leaving only the Bomb spotlit above the altar where no eye could miss it. Brent pulled his eyes away; the dread in his stomach was as tangible as a cancer in its most advanced stage.

Somewhere, the unseen organist struck a note.

From the *prie-dieu*, the kneeling Mendez's voice rose once more:

"Almighty and everlasting Bomb, who came down among us to make Heaven under Earth, lighten our darkness. O instrument of God—Grant us Thy peace."

The organ bleated a series of low, muted chords. All of them climactic, beseeching, uplifting, followed by a final hosannah.

Mendez stood up, back to the congregation, his purple robes a blazing field of color. He raised adoring arms to the Bomb suspended above him. His voice reached up, as if to touch it. To caress it with syllables, words.

The choir's multiple voice rose in song:

"Almighty Bomb—who destroyed Devils—to create Angels! Behold His glory!"

Mendez chimed in with the choir:

"Behold the truth that abides in us, His handicraft!"

The choir stilled and Mendez's chant rose on a single note of prayer and supplication:

"Reveal that truth unto that Maker!"

And now, incredibly, exaltedly, Albina, the fat man, Caspay and the Negro and all the leaders of this ghastly mass stood up as a body and chanted in a synchronized blend of many voices: "*I reveal my Inmost Self unto my God!*"

Brent blinked.

As if he had been struck between the eyes.

Nova shrank against him, mewing like a terrified kitten.

The topmost totem of unreality in this world of un-realities had been reached. Once more the universe had reeled and the mind boggled at what the eyes saw—had to believe—*had* to accept as *Truth*.

All about them, the leaders were unveiling. Albina, the Negro, Caspay, the fat man—everyone. Unmasking, as it were. Pulling and tugging at their heads and faces —taking off rubberized, plasticized masks which had concealed their inmost selves, their *true* appearance. Now Brent and the girl could see in all its blasphe-mous, unmatchable horror the true depths that their nightmare had bought for them when it set them down in this terrible city of lost souls.

Under each mask, each face now revealed to the awful light of the cathedral was a mockery of nature. A countenance repeated endlessly like some hideous joke at a costume party. A face devoid of all hair, all skin, all color and warmth. Centuries of postnuclear mutation had evolved all these faces into skinless hor-rors. Repulsively red and blue and pink, exposing all the ganglia of facial veins, arteries, tendons and muscles. As stripped and visible as any anatomical specimens in a medical class. The leaders, including the mighty Men-dez, were totally horrible, totally and unbelievably hideous.

Brent and Nova held onto each other, shuddering. Mendez exhorted:

"Reveal that truth unto that Maker!"

The choir and the congregation sung back their song of homage:

"*I reveal my Inmost Self unto my God!*"

The congregation now unveiled. The rubbery masks made slithering, uncanny sounds in the stillness of the dark cathedral.

The parody of Life and Nature gleamed from a hun-dred bodies. Brent dared not look too long. His brain was splitting apart again.

And then all the voices raised around him and the girl as the hidden organ swelled into a final exaltation to the devotees of the Bomb Everlasting. Proud and happy voices rose in a tremendous paean of glory: "*All things bright and beautiful, All creatures great and small . . .*"

Caspay smiled in a brotherly fashion at the Negro and then favored Brent with an extension of that smile. But Brent could not in all conscience smile back at that hideous travesty of a human face. He averted his eyes, holding onto Nova's shaking hand.

"*All things wise and wonderful,*" the congregation sang with deep, fervent voices.

The hooded purple head of Mendez turned up to the Bomb again, the spotlit Bomb which looked down on everything. "The good Bomb made us all," the congregation chanted. Some three hundred mutant singers blended into an *intermezzo* between stanzas of the song:

"He gave us eyes to see with, and lips that we might tell How great the Bomb Almighty, who has made all things well. Amen."

During this last *Amen*, Brent saw Albina jerk her weird face at him. The great beauty was a thing of the past. Brent read her message without hearing any words. Unspoken words.

"We can't," he said. "We aren't wearing masks."

She scowled. But Mendez was speaking the Benediction now:

"May the blessing of the Bomb Almighty and the fellowship of the Holy Fallout descend on us all, this night, and for evermore."

Once again he pressed a button on the bejeweled panel board. The emerald one. Even as the congregation's *Amen* died away to a whisper, the spotlight slowly dimmed. The Bomb disappeared into darkness. Fins and all. It was as if it didn't even exist. Had never existed.

Brent kept his arms around Nova. Poor, mute Nova. A waif for all time.

About them, the horrible mutants they had known as the fat man, Caspay, Albina and the Negro, leered hideously. Colors rippled, eddied.

The cathedral throbbed with horror. And the great Unknown.

And Mendez's chants hung in the dim nave, swirling about the high, vaulted reaches of the cathedral. Echoes of Hell and the Pit on all sides. Brent hung onto the little courage left in him.

He had to.

Or there would be no way out.

None at all.

Whatever God's Hell and Damnation was, this had to be it.

For the first time in his life, he had been able to pinpoint the spot. Give it a location.

The Forbidden Zone was Hades, Incorporated.

And this great cathedral was its Limbo.

11   "TAY—LOR!"

The Corridor of Busts, gleaming with its stone gallery honoring the Mendez Dynasty, glimmered like a museum in Brent's eyes. He had been disrobed following the incredible scene in the cathedral so that now he was once more in his familiar rags. Caspay and the Negro were escorting him to some unknown destination. Or fate. Mercifully they had replaced their masks so that their marble faces of beauty were once again intact. Brent wasn't sure he could have borne gazing too long into those skinless, horrendous travesties of the human face. Caspay was smiling, as usual; knowing the man as he now did, Brent knew it meant nothing very good.

"I trust our simple ceremony convinced you of our peaceable intentions," Caspay murmured in his bland way.

"I found it informative," Brent said guardedly.

"Then your cooperation has had its reward."

"Its *only* reward?" Brent turned away from his contemplative study of the busts along the corridor. "When may I hope to be set free?"

Caspay's mouth was still smiling, but not his eyes.

"You may *hope* whenever you please, Mr. Brent. Have pleasant dreams." With that, he waved his hand and continued along the corridor, his green robes rustling.

"I doubt it," Brent answered drily, watching him until he disappeared. The Negro now placed an unwelcome hand on Brent's elbow and guided him to a passage turning left off the corridor's far side. Here, low ceilings and closely distanced walls suggested a catacomb complex. The area was as labyrinthine as a grotto but white-walled and sourcelessly white-lighted. There was no telling where the illumination came from. Brent squinted against the glare.

"How can we let you loose on the eve of a war, Mr. Brent?" the Negro suddenly asked, mildly almost.

Another twist in the labyrinth. Another turn. Brent said nothing.

"You know too many of our secrets," the Negro reminded him.

He halted Brent, for the corridor or passageway had suddenly come to a dead end. A *cul-de-sac* terminating at a closed door that bore no lettering, no identification of any kind. The Negro prodded Brent as he touched a wall button. "Like your friend," he muttered. The door, hinged, opened inward and Brent gaped.

It was a bare white cell, no larger than a storage closet. But within it stood a tall giant of a man. Bearded, bronzed, his great shaggy head oddly in keeping with his garments of loincloth and tatters. The Negro lolled in the doorway, grinning like an ebony idol. Brent staggered forward, his pulse racing, his heart trip-hammering. The bronzed captive in the room blinked back at the open door. At Brent. And then an enormous smile split the almost graven face into a thousand lines of joy and incredible delight.

"Brent!" the giant roared, coming forward.

"TAYLOR!"

Brent fell into his arms, pounding, clapping, babbling excitedly. Taylor clasped him in a bear hug, lifting him off his feet.

The reunion was euphoric.

At first——

The Corridor of Busts echoed with the sound of the guard's heels. Before him, Nova had been moving like a dead woman, her eyes listless and her muscles flaccid. But now, somehow, the shout of Brent's voice echoing the only name she had ever understood came to her, like the call of a bugle. The effect was electrifying. With a wheeling speed more animal than human, she slipped out of the guard's grasp, biting down on his bared hand like a tigress. The guard screamed and let go. Nova broke away from him, running like a gazelle toward the echoes of Brent's cry. And the sound of the name, *Tay-lor!*

Before the guard could rally in lumbering pursuit, his damaged hand already bleeding, the girl had sprinted down the corridor, turned into the passage leading to the catacomb complex and vanished from sight.

Nova ran like the wind.

The guard pounded along behind her.

Her bared feet made slapping noises along the passageway floor.

"How the hell did you get here?" Taylor demanded. They had both simmered down from the unbounded joy of meeting again and were now both of them well aware of the tall Negro still positioned in the doorway. Brent forced a smile. The white of the cell was a glare.

"I came by subway, naturally."

"You're two thousand years late," Taylor replied through cracked lips. His heroic face, which would have looked so proper on a coin or medallion, had always pleased the younger man.

"Service never was much good," Brent agreed.

"Is your commander with you?"

"He's dead. Went blind—and blew a lung on re-entry."

Taylor sighed. "Then how . . . ?"

"Nova found me."

"*She's* here?" Taylor started forward, his big shoulders flexing. "Where is she?"

"They separated us—thank God."

"Why thank God?"

"They were trying to make me kill her——" Suddenly, he stared at Taylor. "Come to that, why haven't they killed *you?*"

From the doorway, the Negro's voice lilted pleasantly in reply.

"You know why, Mr. Brent. We're a peaceful people. We don't kill our enemies." Taylor and Brent saw his beatific smile. "We get our enemies to kill each other." The Negro paused, then directed his next remark to Taylor. "It takes two to make a quarrel. With whom could you quarrel, Mr. Taylor, *while you were alone?*"

Brent shuddered, knowing what that could mean.

Taylor didn't. He advanced belligerently on the Negro, hands bunching.

"I don't know what you're talking about!" he snarled, showing the erosion that imprisonment had worked on him and his will power.

"But I do," Brent said. "Unfortunately."

The Negro closed his eyes.

Brent braced himself, steeling his will against the mental assault he knew was underway. Taylor gawked at him, puzzled. The gawk widened as he saw Brent's hands come up, fashion themselves into fists. Brent had assumed an aggressive, fighting position! He could see the perspiration breaking out on Brent's face. But, in-credibly—impossibly—*his own hands were coming up, knotting into fists*, and he felt his brain grow cold with hate and the desire to crush, hurt, maim.

Taylor confronted Brent.

Brent confronted Taylor.

The Negro, eyes still closed, remained in the door-way.

The glare of the cell was white, stark, ugly.

The smiles had drained from the two astronauts. Both faces began to twitch under the hammer blows of hypnosis.

Vainly resisting, Brent gasped, "I am fighting an order! I . . . am . . . fighting . . . a FRIEND!"

With that, he lashed out with a terrible left to the jutting promontory of Taylor's chin.

The fight was vicious, savage.

Both men, friends, in the grip of a power willing them not merely to hurt, but to murder each other—with no lethal holds barred and no dirty killer's tricks left untried—collided in the center of the room. Taylor gouged at Brent's eyes. Brent swung a violent foot into Taylor's groin. The sound of the encounter was pro-digious. They locked in the death grip of brutal close combat. Kicking, gouging, biting, clawing, tearing at each other like two wild animals. Grunts, groans and curses filled the cell. The Negro, eyes screwed tightly shut, stood unmoving in the doorway. His face might have been carved out of marble.

Taylor caught Brent in a powerful viselike hold, swung him like a rag doll and then battered him with his head, butting like a ram. Brent kicked out with his legs. He caught Taylor in the pit of the stomach. Taylor let go and Brent broke loose. For a long second both men were free of each other, circling warily, waiting for the next opening. Their faces were bloody masks, their teeth exposed in brutal animal snarls. They were all but spitting at one another. The savage code of the jungle. Survival of the fittest, the law of fang and claw. They were slavering, gasping and grunting. Two mockeries of intelligent life.

The Negro, eyes still shut, dug into his white robes and produced two weapons. Two shining short knives with hafts of ebony. These he threw unseeing into the center of the room. The knives clattered onto the floor. As if they had been thrown a bone, Taylor and Brent instantly swept up the weapons. Now the fight assumed a deadlier overtone. An aura of the slaughter house hung about the cell, a charnel atmosphere which had eons and eras of brutality, prehistoric violence and unthinking savagery as its questionable guide.

Brent and Taylor went at each other still more viciously.

There was the sharp, ringing strike of metal against metal, the fierce muted thunder of men breathing like animals, gulping oxygen with bestial rapidity. Snarling, snapping, biting, digging at one another as if the universe depended on this one single encounter to give anything of life meaning, sense.

The Negro stood through it all, back against the door, holding it open, silently waiting for the outcome that had to be the death of one or both men. The stunning waves of traumatic hypnosis held Brent and Taylor in a dazzling, relentless hold which would not loosen until the Negro opened his eyes.

The barren little cell permitted no escape. No headway. No room in which to maneuver to advantage. Like the suicidal duels of ancient times, both combatants were committed to a battle from which neither could possibly emerge unscathed or unmarked. Blood would tell.

It was falling now, spurting from cuts and slices and minor wounds which only served to make Brent and Taylor go at each other all the stronger with their lunging, stabbing thrusts. The Negro maintained his position.

And the outcome drew nearer.

Inevitable, like something preordained.

The fight was now at its sharpest pitch.

There was about it that ferocity that lent it an animal quality. Except that it was easier to kill with a knife than to rend and tear a man to bloody fragments.

Brent moved like a ferret, hacking out at the bigger man.

He made a score. Blood spurted from Taylor's side as the knife bit in and pulled out again.

Taylor roared from deep in his chest, bounded forward, and Brent found himself face to face with finality. Now the death dance began, with the two of them reeling around the narrow white cell, knives going for each other's bared throats; then hand to hand, each holding onto the enemy knife aimed now at his own heart.

And then there was an interruption.

Nova materialized in the door behind the Negro.

She saw Taylor, saw the fight. The shock and the joy combined in one mammoth surge of emotion that needed some outlet, some vent through which to escape. Some avenue along which to meet the world.

The miracle occurred.

Nova's neck muscles arched, her lips parted and she spoke.

The name.

The magic word.

"Tay-lor . . ."

The word was tinny, faint, a faraway sound but as crystal-clear in quality as the first word spoken by a schooled deaf child. As can happen with a mute who is not necessarily deaf, the girl had managed the very first word of her life.

And Taylor heard her.

And Brent heard her.

And, fatally for him, the Negro also heard her. He made the mistake of *opening his eyes.*

Brent sobbed, the magical change sweeping over his brain.

"His eyes are open."

Taylor staggered back, equally freed of the mental lock. Brent jumped forward, knife upraised, and plunged the point of the blade into the Negro's heart. The white-robed figure threshed against the door, then lurched forward into the cell. Brent watched, panting. The knife protruded from the reddening folds of the white robe. The Negro plucked at it ineffectually, his hands pawing feebly. Away from the door, his weight free of it, the barrier swung shut with a slam. There was no handle on the inner side of the cell. Brent was too late to catch the door before it closed. There was the click of an automatic lock.

Eyes glazed, the Negro blurted, "Unto God . . . I reveal . . ." His bloodstained hands tore at the rubberized mask of his features, "my Inmost S-s-s-se . . ."

He fell flat on his face before he could complete the gesture. Taylor, bathed in sweat, crouched over his prostrate body, his eyes almost insane. Brent suddenly retched; a ratchety cough of pain. Taylor went to him, seeing the widening stain of blood from a place in Brent's shoulder where his own knife had drawn blood. Nova had come forward to assist him, both of them trying to stanch the flow of red from Brent's wound. It was an awesome slice across the deltoid. Taylor quickly cut strips from the dead Negro's white robe to fashion a crude but serviceable bandage. Brent winced painfully. Taylor worked fast, conscious of Nova hovering at his side. The girl was smiling despite everything.

"You talked," Taylor said simply, kissing her gently. "And we're alive."

She looked up at him, pleased at his evident pleasure. Then he kissed her again. A prolonged kiss. Brent smiled, but in the sudden silence he could hear a soft but steady rush of sound. Like—*air!* Coming from— Brent's eyes searched the room rapidly—there was a six-inch impenetrably grilled vent in the wall behind Taylor, just above his head. Taylor broke from the kiss.

"It's no use," he told Brent, quick to the direction of his gaze. "I've tried. We're near a main air-conditioning vent."

"It's cold," Brent said.

Taylor eyed the inert body of the Negro with distaste.

"Just as well." His nose wrinkled. "We may have to wait, and I'm allergic to the stink of death. Now, talk some more, Brent. And make it quick."

Brent fingered his bandage, fighting the pain.

"They have an atom bomb."

Taylor's eyes narrowed. "Operational?"

"Yes. And they intend to use it."

"What type is it?"

"That's just it—I don't know. It belongs to a series I've never seen before. Maybe because I don't have top clearance as yet." This last was almost rueful.

"I do," Taylor said grimly.

"Or did," Brent tried a small joke. Gallows humor. "Two thousand years ago."

Taylor wasn't listening.

"Did you see a series number?"

"Yes—on one of the fins. Except there were no numbers. Just two Greek letters. *Alpha, omega.*"

Taylor's face tightened into a mask of inner pain. "May God help us," he said in a low voice.

Brent started. "What is it? What does it mean?"

"Doomsday Bomb," Taylor said. "Cobalt casing. The last we ever made. Only one. One was enough. The idea was to threaten the enemy by the very fact that it existed. A bomb so powerful it could destroy—not just a city—not just a nation—no, not just every living cell on earth, every insect, every blade of grass—but set nuclear fire to the wind, to the air itself. Scorch the whole planet into a cinder! Like the end of a burnt match. The ultimate bomb——" His voice trailed off into a whisper.

Nova, always responsive to his moods, huddled closer to him.

Brent had forgotten all about the throbbing discomfort of his damaged shoulder.

The baffled guard who had allowed Nova to elude him was still searching for her. Without any success. He had not entered the catacomb complex but had returned to the Corridor of Busts to make a fresh start on his hunt. He was startled to see someone in the renowned corridor. Somebody wise and all-powerful.

Mendez in his purple robes was kneeling before the stoic bust of MENDEZ I. He was silent and immobile. As if his entire being was as one with his legendary ancestor.

Mendez seemed to commune with the inanimate bust.

The guard withdrew very carefully, anxious not to make a whisper of sound. He stole up the long corridor like a wraith.

The posture of the leader disturbed the guard.

Was something wrong that Mendez had to take this time to pray on the eve of a great conflict?

But the guard removed the thought from his already worried mind. There was still the girl to find . . .

Angrily, impatiently, the guard moved down the corridor past the closed doors of the Inquisition Room.

Nothing stirred.

Not even the kneeling figure of Mendez behind him, beyond the turn of the passageway.

12   DR. ZAIUS

The Grand Army of the Apes had achieved the frontier zone of the designated area. Now, as the hot sun beat down in a cobalt-blue sky, General Ursus initiated the opening steps of the invasion. Beyond the burning rim of the horizon, the skyline of buried New York steepled eerily. Silhouetted and somber. From his horse, with Zaius at his side, Ursus' medals shone in the sunlight. He raised a glittering sword.

His army moved. Quickly, in full military pomp and precision. Orders were shouted, marching feet thundered, equipment rolled into position. Squadrons formed. Gorilla infantry, about fifty apes to each group, with a commissioned officer and a noncommissioned officer leading every command, flanked into attacking formation. The gun carriages wheeled up, clanking noisily. Bayonets gleamed from rifle tips. The assembled apes were ready to attack. To fight. To obey the Ursus dictim of *Invade, Invade, Invade!* Dr. Zaius looked on almost sorrowfully at the spectacle of force of arms triumphing over sober reflection and discourse with the enemy. Ursus, eyes shaded against the sun, peering toward New York in the distance, summoned a bugler to his side. His gimlet eyes were twin pools of ecstasy. His black gorilla face was exalted. The morning heat set a shimmering haze over the scene. It was a lovely day for the Invasion.

"Sound the advance," Ursus commanded the bugler in the sudden total hush that preceded the strike of lightning forces from the kingdom of Ape City.

The horn brayed, a pealing blast of sound wafting over the formation. The army, in extended order, advanced. *Uphill.* Toward the visible reaches of the Forbidden Zone. Ursus' mount pranced in the vanguard. Zaius trotted along behind him.

The hill was steep, sloping upward at a hazardous angle. The ape army swarmed upward, a vast body of moving gorillas, horses and ordnance. With skilled coordination of all units and a minimum of stumbling blocks, the advance platoons of Ursus' forces gained the crest of the mountain which overlooked the buried grandeur of New York.

Ursus reached the pinnacle first. Then Zaius, then the troops directly behind them. Ursus lifted a paw to signal a halt. The army came to a stop. Waiting legions, motionless in the sun.

Zaius' breath caught in his chest. Ursus groaned mightily.

The spectacle before them defied belief.

Where before there had been nothing but limitless expanses of arid desert in the vast sun-bleached acreage leading to buried New York, there was now nothing but horror.

Row upon row of naked gorillas, hanging from inverted crosses staked to the ground, glowed wickedly in the sunlight. A mass crucifixion, awesome in all its implications, to match the Roman massacre of Christians along the Appian Way in another equally terrible time. Zaius' scholarly blood ran cold. Ursus' face darkened. Fire and smoke, both sourceless and spread out like a blaze encompassing the world, had also appeared, seemingly from nowhere. And still the mutilated gorillas hung crucified from their upside-down crosses.

The ape army, particularly the infantry, closest to the sight, aghast and quivering in horror at the devastation below them, began to panic. A great tumult of shouting and anguished cries went up. Ursus, livid with rage, found himself being berated by Dr. Zaius.

"Ursus, I warned you! Look what we are faced with! I told you we should wait!"

"Whoever did this," Ursus growled, "will pay heavily."

The groans of the crucified gorillas were clamorous, rising from the bloody desert plain like a universal wail of misery, sorrow and agony. Dr. Zaius shuddered, reining in his horse.

"If you have any pity, order your soldiers to shoot our people."

"I cannot order what the Lawgiver has forbidden. Ape shall not kill Ape," Ursus snarled, wheeling his mount to shout an order to one of his nearest commanders. "Prepare to attack!"

"Attack what and whom?" Zaius demanded softly, his orangutan face constricted in lines of bewilderment and compassion.

The ape army suddenly rallied.

Gorillas, horses and guns moved up over the ridge, pounding over the crest, swarming down the other side. Ursus led the way. The infantry rushed forward, racing across the desert to the grim spectacle of their slaughtered comrades. Shouts and gunfire filled the air. Gorillas yelled and screamed, summoning up a *banzai*-like courage to grope with the situation. Or cope. The hot sun blazed down, as if trying to pierce the gathering smoke and fire filling the landscape. The infantry rushed. Ursus spurred his mount. Zaius galloped alongside.

And then . . .

A colossal effigy of the Lawgiver, the Great Ape reading a book, materialized in view, his stone feet among the scorching flames, his head seeming to touch the sky. The apes in the oncoming infantry group braked to a halt. Utter consternation and dread took over where before nothing but fear had ruled. These emotions—and a great joy!

"The Lawgiver!" a gorilla soldier squealed in delight. He dropped his rifle and kneeled. The soldier beside him, humbled by the vision of ape greatness, cried out, "He will avenge our crucified brothers!"

"Vengeance!" shouted the next soldier.

And the cry was taken up by the rest of the ape infantry. A mighty chorus of adulation, happiness and sheer exaltation echoed over the scene. Baffled by what he saw, General Ursus roared at all of his commanders, "Hold your positions!"

The gigantic figure of the Lawgiver now seemed to show the many holes and perforations in his great body. From these openings, red blood flowed in a scarlet spiderweb of color. Pumping, welling, spurting terribly. Ursus, in fear and horror, had to cling to his mount for support, his eyes two black marbles of disbelief. The Lawgiver, the Almighty, the Great One, the Nonpareil, the Master of all Apes, was bleeding to death before his very eyes!

"He bleeds!" General Ursus boomed. "The Lawgiver bleeds!"

An atavistic growl thundered from his chest; a trumpeting blast of animal sound that must have echoed in the days when his ancestors swung from trees and loped along the ground for their food. As for the ape infantry, it was completely demoralized by the spectacle. They threw down their rifles, pointing and gibbering with dismay at the Thing In The Sky. Simian cries of alarm and dismay rose in a blended medley of vocal terror that sounded exactly like the monkey house in a twentieth-century zoo. Above the blasted, cursed desert, the effigy of the Lawgiver, flung there by the hypnotic powers of the leaders of the Forbidden Zone, continued to bleed to death.

Only Dr. Zaius was able to retain his wits, to keep his head. The fufillment of all his hopes for a compromise of the minds hung on the action he was now steeling himself to take. Turning, he faced the paralyzed, screaming infantry of gorillas and raised his cultured voice to an unfamiliar authoritative shout.

"The spirit of the Lawgiver lives! We are still God's chosen! And this is a vision and it is a lie!"

Before they could digest his words, he charged. Alone. On horseback. Out toward the bleeding image of the Lawgiver. The astounded gorillas quietened, stunned by the sight of the old scientist, the Minister of Science, galloping out toward his inevitable doom.

Dr. Zaius rode into the Vision.

Rode out between the row upon row of crucified apes. Past the inverted crosses, through the veritable forest of slaughter—toward the Effigy of the Lawgiver. His horse shied and whinnied but Zaius kept a tight rein. Soon the clattering hooves had led him up to the vision. The smoke and the flame. The scorching fingers of the blaze eating away at the very feet of the Lawgiver.

Behind him, General Ursus and the Grand Army of the Apes looked on in mounting wonder.

Zaius' horse reared, kicking at the smoke and the flame.

The Vision.

And slowly, inexorably, the Vision toppled, falling down, hitting the sandy earth. It exploded with great violence, creating a huge sheet of flame and roaring black smoke.

The entire tableau vanished in an instant.

And then—suddenly—the smoke was gone. The flame was gone. So was the image of the Lawgiver. And the forest of crucified apes. There was nothing on the vast, empty, rocky and sandy landscape but the figures of Dr. Zaius and his horse. Everything had faded away, leaving only what was really true and the reality that was really there.

General Ursus, staggered, and insanely jealous of Zaius for doing what he should have done, could only gaze on the scene with utter wonder and regret for a marvelous opportunity lost. One that he would never have again.

Dr. Zaius had passed through the Vision, triumphed over it. In the name of his science. He turned and waved to the Army of Ursus. There was nothing interposed between him and his people on the slope of the hill. The stage of desert and landscape was desolate.

General Ursus reformed his army.

He coldly acknowledged the signals of his revitalized commanders and troops. Dr. Zaius remained where he was, waiting for the Grand Army to rejoin him. Ursus' color was malignant. He was furious. It was Zaius, and not he, whose gallant action had turned the tide of battle. Mottled, Ursus summoned the bugler again.

"Sound the advance," he said dully.

Once more the braying notes of the horn filtered out over the baked panorama of landscape. In the visible distance the steeples and tombstone tops of New York lay illuminated in the sun. The tips of the Empire

State, the Chrysler Building—and the face of Miss Liberty poking from the earth like a milestone—stood like markers along the route. General Ursus dug his spurs into his horse's flanks and raced out to join Dr. Zaius where he still waited. A solitary figure on the desert plain.

Damn the good doctor!

There would be no living with the orangutan now . . .

The Grand Army of the Apes moved out toward the city on the horizon.

In the Inquisition Room, Mendez and his surviving inquisitors, seated on their curved chairs, had their eyes focused on the opposite wall level with their heads. Caspay, the fat man and Mendez, projecting purple, green and red, were throwing mental images to keep themselves abreast of the military situation. Albina's blue was negative.

Which was critical now.

They saw General Ursus and Dr. Zaius, at the head of the Grand Army of the Apes, defeat the specter of the desert, move into the city and press onward. Zaius' face appeared on the wall. Dismounted from his horse, he was pointing to the ground, calling Ursus' attention to a six-foot-square octagonal vent just beyond his horse's hooves. The same octagonal vent which had guided Brent and Nova into the very heart of the metropolis.

"*There are ways down*," Zaius was shouting.

The perfect color on the wall dissolved as Mendez and Caspay and the fat man rose from their chairs. Mendez's smooth face was calm but his eyes moved strangely. Flakes of gold in a mysterious wind of inner turmoil.

Caspay addressed the fat man.

"You know the range of their city?"

The red-clad fat man nodded.

"Set it in the mechanism and wait for me."

The fat man left the Inquisition Room.

Caspay smiled at the beautiful Albina.

"I want a public thought projection at adult and infant level. *'Clear the streets. Stay indoors.'*"

Albina nodded too. Then she also rustled out of the room.

"What will you do, Holiness?" Caspay asked Mendez.

Mendez's marble face was fixed with confident placidity.

"Everything necessary," he murmured.

Caspay smiled his benevolent puckish smile and fondled his green robes.

All would be well, no matter how well organized and powerful the ape army might be.

There was still the Almighty Bomb!

And Mendez, whose brilliance outshone even the sun.

The last of the ape infantrymen had clambered down into the six main vents. Nothing remained on the surface of the Forbidden Zone but endless scores of tethered horses, waiting patiently for the eventual return of their riders. Four young gorilla sentries guarded the mounts as the main force pushed on.

An aura of excitement prevailed.

General Ursus and Dr. Zaius led the way along the narrow, glaringly white passageway. The cool air, the almost antiseptic texture of the corridor fascinated Zaius but Ursus could now smell blood. His gorilla face was beaming with expectancy. The unexpected rise of Zaius to hero status no longer disturbed him. There would be fresh battles, new conquests, and soon! He could almost feel the proximity of combat, the matching of arms with this rabble who had to live underground like worms and play tricks with gorilla minds. Well, he would show them. Show Zaius too. Show everybody—the unimpeachable wisdom of *Invade, Invade, Invade!*

Everything was going so smoothly now.

Once out of this damnable corridor, they would come face to face with the half savages who had dared to mock gorilla might and abuse gorilla people.

Yes, he would show them.

Show everybody.

The ineluctable power of *Force.*

There was just no other way to run a country. A people. A civilization. Foolish man had learned that, hadn't he, to his sorrow. Trying to rule a world with the milk of kindness.

Damn chimpanzee philosophy.

Weak-kneed, thin-skinned. Hopelessly . . .

Grunting happily, his eyes shining, General Ursus moved down the long shining corridor at the head of his troops.

Dr. Zaius tagged along, just behind him.

Zaius was still unhappy.

He did not like the signs all around them of a vastly superior race of beings.

A race of intellects.

For which no gorilla could ever be a match.

Beyond the maze of octagonal corridors, in the cold glare of the metropolis above, nothing moved on the streets of the Forbidden Zone. There was a curious, almost frightening emptiness to the streets. No little knots of playing children, no passers-by, no single solitary streetwalkers. Nobody.

Only the wind fanning eerily over the half-buried building tops, the windowless structures which resembled so many headstones and tombstones jutting from the depths of the faraway mountains.

Only the mammoth silhouette of the great cathedral poking into the slate-gray skies.

The cathedral that housed the Bomb.

The Almighty Bomb.

Dedicated to the Holy Fallout.

And ultimate Oblivion.

13   APE AND MAN

"They're coming," Brent said.

Outside their cell, they could hear the thunderous united tramp of marching feet. The sudden rumble of movement and equipment moved Taylor faster than any warning could have. Quickly he lugged the corpse of the Negro to the base of the cell wall. Brent and Nova joined him there, flattening out along the ground, hugging the wall. Out of sight of the peephole in the door of the cell.

A helmeted gorilla face loomed there.

He couldn't see Taylor, Brent and the girl, or the Negro lying directly below him out of his line of sight. The gorilla face winced briefly and then the black muzzle of a machine gun appeared, poking into the cell.

The weapon stuttered, erupted, blasted and raked the interior of the cell with lateral fire. The stench of cordite filled the room. Soon the firing ceased and the gorilla moved on, joining the tramping hordes in the corridor. Not until the sound of marching feet diminished did Taylor, Brent or Nova move.

"Wait," cautioned Brent.

They didn't know that Company A of the ape army had just trooped by their place of confinement.

The marching sounds faded into silence.

Taylor rose to his feet, picking up a club which lay in one corner of the cell. He used this now to batter away at the cell door, smashing it open with a burst of tremendous blows. Brent's bandages were oozing blood. He was sweating and his face was gray with pain. Taylor hesitated, but peered down the corridor beyond the battered door. Then he looked at Brent. Brent looked at him. Each man in that instant recognized what the other had in mind. Nova stood, waiting eternally, as she always had to, with her men.

"Let's go!" Brent snapped impatiently. "Let's go!"

Taylor nodded, and let Brent push into the corridor. He took Nova's hand and led her out.

The corridor was empty.

Taylor eyed Brent with fresh respect.

"You've got the same crazy thought I have, haven't you?"

"Except, it's not crazy," Brent panted, the pain searing him. "If these—'people'—think they're going to lose to the apes, they'll explode the bomb. Which is the end of the apes, but also the end of everything else. The end of life. The end of the world. You told me that yourself."

"I should do it alone," Taylor said.

"Let's double our chances."

Taylor frowned. "I don't know if you're much use. You're bleeding pretty good . . ."

"I'm all right!"

Before Taylor could answer that, a sound of gunfire hammered near them and they heard the hoarse screams of some gorilla soldiers. Taylor jumped. He had caught sight of three gorilla soldiers coming down the passageway. He backed quickly into the cell, pulling Nova with him. Too late. They had been seen. With a whoop of something akin to pleasure, the gorillas bounded forward, weapons upraised. Obviously, they had already had some casualties and this was a chance to even up a few scores. Grimly, Taylor and Brent braced to meet the attack. Taylor had his club; Nova shrank into one corner of the cell.

The fight was brief and bloody.

Brent and Taylor, motivated by a tremendous fear and a desire for survival, swarmed over the gorilla trio. Taylor swung the heavy club with telling accuracy. But as the scuffle ensued and Brent chipped in as best he could, one of the gorilla rifles got off a random shot. Soon, however, his face a contorted mask, Taylor won the day. The club smashed out, battering gorilla heads and faces. Suddenly the corridor was a pile of inert soldiers. Taylor swayed, panting from the effort. And then he turned back to Nova and Brent, almost smiling.

The smile vanished.

Nova lay crumpled on the floor of the cell. Her slender, lithe body did not move. There was an ugly stain spreading over the pitiful rags that covered her left breast.

She was dead. The random shot had found her as truly as any marksman's well-aimed bullet.

The face of Taylor crumpled. Strength fled from it. He moved to the girl, fell to his knees, cradling her still head in his lap. Brent stood by, helpless. The moment held, Taylor holding the girl, silently dying within himself. Then he stood up, his dirty, bronzed face flooded with an almost uncontrollable anger. Beyond the walls of the cell, the sounds of street combat echoed dimly.

"I should let them all die!" Taylor raged, his voice rising on a sob. "Not just the gorillas! Everyone! Every living thing! Us too! Look at how it all ends——! It's time it was finished——finished!"

He clawed at the air, a monument of bitterness and frustration. His great body trembled.

"Come on, Taylor," Brent spoke up, more strongly than before, trying not to think about Nova. About anything that had to do with love and gentleness. "Come on!"

He moved out of the cell, not looking back.

Not daring to recall.

Forgetting Nova and her mute, appealing goodness.

He knew that Taylor would follow him.

Taylor the man had to.

Taylor did.

But Taylor was remembering . . .

His brain was alive with images. Swirling, exploding pictures of the grand error which had begun with a space flight from Cape Kennedy. The disastrous flight, the time differential, the coming down into the smooth blue lake in the middle of nowhere. The death of the woman astronaut, shriveled like a mummy on landing. The planting of the small American flag in the middle of nowhere. The capture by the apes; the lobotomizing of one of the others. His own escape from Ape City with the help of a beautiful savage girl who had trusted him from the very beginning. Without words, without complaints. The sight of the Statue of Liberty poking from the sands, the wall of ice and—losing the girl. Finding himself here in this underground civilization of mutants.

And Cornelius, Zira and Dr. Zaius.

And now Brent, a man from that same world that had vanished. Brent—almost the reflection of himself. What he had once been, at any rate.

And Nova . . .

Nova!

By God, he had loved her. More than any woman he ever knew back on the planet in the time when all men hoped for the best in order to avoid the worst.

His eyes hardened into flints. His tears dried up.

This world, whatever it was, *would have to pay for Nova!*

B, C and D Company of the ape army had solved the various complexities of the many and different air tunnels leading into the center of the leaders' domain. All companies, jubilant, armed and prepared for slaughter, moved in for the kill.

From convergent directions.

General Ursus' militia was functioning like a well-oiled machine. Victory was in sight.

In the Corridor of Busts, Dr. Zaius stood staring at the impressive rows of sculpted heads depicting the Mendez Dynasty. His intelligent nostrils were curled in disgust. He looked down the row of busts on their plinths and saw where the Inquisition Room began. The door. The bust of Mendez I heightened Zaius' distaste.

With Zaius was a gorilla sergeant, machine gun at the ready. Ursus had gone off somewhere, with bigger plans in his head. Zaius shivered, looking at the stone idols. "They're obscene," he muttered. The sergeant made no comment, but kept his eyes peeled, on the alert.

Zaius suddenly knocked Mendez I off his gleaming plinth. The bust crashed to the floor, shattering. Methodically, grimly, Dr. Zaius moved down the line, striking out, pushing, breaking. One by one, the stone history of the Mendez Dynasty broke apart in scattered, useless fragments. With great enthusiasm, Zaius finally reached the end of the stone line. Mendez XXVI. The last bust disintegrated on the floor in a shower of chips.

As it too smashed, a woman's scream, muffled but agonizing, sounded from beyond the door of the Inquisition Room.

The sergeant brushed by Dr. Zaius, batted the wall button and plunged in. Zaius followed him, curious.

They found Albina.

She lay sprawled in her lovely blue robes in a curved chair before the wall screen. A small phial was clutched in her outstretched hand. Her lovely face, even in death, was as stunningly beautiful as ever. Zaius scooped up the phial, put it to his nose and sniffed. The sergeant could not take his eyes off the beauty of Albina nor the ample spill of her nearly bared breasts in the blue robes. She was still bewitching.

"She's dead," Zaius said, without inflection.

He turned away, leaving the sergeant to ogle Albina while he studied the strange room. The wall caught his interest . . .

When he turned back it was to see the sergeant's hairy paw on Albina's unmoving breast. The sergeant was greatly agitated, sexually stimulated. Zaius hid his disgust for all gorillas. *Animals!*

"Sergeant," he said mildly.

The ape withdrew his hand.

Dr. Zaius continued to study the Inquisition Room.

There was a lot to be learned here.

He could see that, too.

The great double doors of the cathedral reverberated with the crescendo thud of an ape-wielded battering ram. General Ursus stood back as his armed troops broke down the mighty doors. In the cathedral square, ape companies had converged until they now totaled nearly three hundred strong. General Ursus was proud and happy. Victory was in the air.

The war was going well!

There had been an interesting diversion on the way to the cathedral. A bit of sport. For himself and his gorilla squads of highly efficient soldiers.

In the stone plaza outside the church, they had en-

countered three robed figures hurrying across the
square. A huge fat man encased in scarlet robes, an
elder-statesman type in brilliant green, and a tall, lean,
hooded man. These had been, of course, the fat man,
Caspay and the verger. General Ursus had not even
bothered to halt them to ask questions. Rather, he had
raised one authoritative paw and the machine gunners
flanking him had done their specialty. A withering,
blasting, raking crossfire of a thousand bullets which
had seemed to pluck up the robed figures and send
them skittering like puppets along the hard earth until
the guns had closed down. General Ursus had never
seen, in all his military past, such effectiveness of machine gun fire on mere flesh. The dull, bleak buildings
bordering the plaza, with their curious starkness and
contrasting moldiness and fresh stone architecture, had
shown no signs of life. The streets and the alleys of
this tomblike metropolis had been curiously empty.

Save for the three hurrying figures in robes.

General Ursus had not been disposed to take them
prisoner to ask them questions. He somehow felt that
the imposing edifice of the cathedral held all the answers he might need to know.

In any case, the machine gun exercise had been a
necessary tactic for his troops. Lest their fingers grow
stale from disuse.

Ursus hardly gave the bullet-riddled, blood-soaked
corpses a second look as he trundled up to the mighty
double doors at the head of his troops. He felt an
imminent end to this war.

Genuine resistance had been virtually nil. These
people, whatever they were, were certainly no
warriors!

He had waited for Dr. Zaius to join him at this hour
of ultimate conquest. Still smarting from the heroics
of Zaius on the plain, before the whole of his Grand

Army, Ursus was anxious to get some of his own back. And now was the time.

The great doors of the cathedral unhinged, broken open by the force of the ram. General Ursus and his troops piled through the new opening. Dr. Zaius accompanied them.

With nearly three hundred elite gorilla troops behind him, General Ursus stalked into the cathedral proudly. Mightily. The great dim hall lay in gloom. Only the half light of the *prie-dieu* on the high altar showed any illumination. Ursus moved toward this, his troops and Zaius following. Their feet made gobbling echoes in the gigantic nave.

There was only one man in the cathedral.

Mendez. The Twenty-Sixth.

Dr. Zaius recognized the glasslike, marble-like face.

The altar screens were closed behind Mendez. In his purple robes, Mendez awaited his conquerors.

Ursus and Zaius, flanked by gorilla machine gunners, stalked up the nave to a point midway where Ursus imperiously motioned for a halt. Mendez did not move. His face was impassive in the dim light.

"Arrest that—creature," Ursus commanded the guards. "And bring it to me."

The guards moved forward, machine guns leveled, reaching the sanctuary.

Behind the *prie-dieu*, Mendez pressed the emerald button on the panel board. It glowed green.

The altar screens parted noiselessly. The guards looked up, hesitating. And in the moment of their indecision, Mendez's powerful voice filled the cathedral, echoing off the vaulted ceiling.

"*This is the instrument of my God.*"

The first guard recoiled, batting his eyes at his partner.

"He can speak!"

Mendez pressed the second button on the bejeweled panel. The topaz one. It glowed yellow.

General Ursus snorted, angry with the delay. He started forward, snarling, "Your God . . . !"

Spurred by his voice, the guards seized Mendez, attempting to drag him off the high altar. Zaius caught his breath in a gasp of wonderment. And new knowledge.

The Bomb was in view.

Resplendent, frightening, all mighty, its sinister fins and snoutlike nose magnificently awesome. It had begun to *rise*—very very slowly, in response to the mechanism triggered by the topaz button. And now, as it would have been obvious to Taylor and Brent, the Bomb was poising itself on a mammoth launching pad.

The steel sides of the monster glistened out over the cathedral. Mendez began to raise his own arms in genuflection and homage. General Ursus' face twisted with sheer rage and hate.

"Your God didn't save you, did he?" he snarled, motioning to the soldiers. Before Mendez could speak again, the guards has brutally knotted the purple robes about his defenseless throat, and with both of them vising from each side, had strangled him where he stood. It took only two minutes. Mendez flopped like a limp doll when they finally released him, falling to the floor of the high altar. Ursus laughed sardonically at the sight.

Then he snatched a machine gun from one of the guards and aimed it up at the Bomb. Directly at the glistening metallic body of the thing. Dr. Zaius moved quickly, speaking in a furious undertone. "Ursus, you fool! That's a weapon built by Man . . ."

Ursus spat full in his face.

Zaius was heedless of that. He gestured at the Bomb suspended on the launching pad.

"You can't shoot it down with a clip of bullets!"

Ursus sneered. He was a simple soldier. The Devil take Zaius and his intellectual claptrap! He tugged back the cocking handle of the machine gun with one black paw. His gimlet eyes were beady with joy.

"It'll kill us all—" Zaius begged, trying to knock the gun aside. Ursus growled, pushed him aside, leveled the machine gun upward and fired. The cathedral rocked with the sounds of automatic fire. Ursus kept on firing until the machine gun closed down on an empty drum of cartridges. His face was angry again.

The impenetrable armor plating of the Bomb had deflected all the bullets of the bursting gunfire. Ricochets had whined and howled all over the nave. General Ursus flung the machine gun back to its owner. He brushed his paws together. His troops were still waiting, crowded behind him in this enemy cathedral.

"Well, if we can't shoot it down, we'll haul it down. Rope and tackle!" he bellowed in a voice used to giving commands and being obeyed. Zaius fell back gratefully. All was not yet lost.

Thirty soldiers came forward, put down their weapons and mounted the high altar, making preparations to do as the General ordered. Thirty apes began to climb up the great golden brackets that supported the Bomb. They climbed agilely, quickly, efficiently.

As only apes can.

General Ursus waited, smiling.

Dr. Zaius could only hope for the best.

At the dark end of the cathedral, behind the massed troops at the edge of the battered double doors, with the diversion of the activity on the high altar aiding their surreptitious entrance, Taylor and Brent crept into view.

Their faces were damp, strained and unearthly.

Their eyes could have belonged to madmen.

Far away in Ape City, the house of Zira and Cornelius had grown unaccountably colder. Cornelius checked the barometer on the kitchen wall. He frowned. Almost perfect for the season—then why was the place so drafty? It wasn't at all logical.

Zira came in from the living room, her cute nuzzle wrinkling.

"Well?" she asked, hugging her forearms.

Cornelius shrugged. "Doesn't make sense. Shouldn't be cold at all. Not for this time of year."

Zira shuddered. Her tiny eyes sparkled.

"Maybe it's an omen," she laughed. "That things aren't going so well for our glorious ape army."

"Zira," Cornelius said wearily.

"Oh, you!" she raged suddenly. "You'll never do anything about anything, will you?"

Cornelius had nothing to say to that.

Nor did the house get any warmer as daylight waned.

No word had come, as yet, from the Forbidden Zone.

14   BOMB

The attention of the cathedral was solely on the act being performed on the bomb. Zaius, Ursus and the others were all intent on the ape soldiers clambering aloft, scrambling all over the steel sides of the monster. A network of ropes had been slung around the weapon so that the apes could now haul at the rising Bomb. With great strength and celerity, the soldiers tugged at the ropes. The Bomb stopped.

Ursus smiled triumphantly at Zaius.

"Well done!" he bellowed to his troops.

Now the Bomb, still carrying the clinging, climbing apes, was pulled down to the ground. It lay dormant, off the launching pad. Zaius almost shrugged. Yet, he was still worried.

At the rear of the gloom-shrouded cathedral, Brent moved painfully down the left side of the aisle, making full use of the cathedral's architectural covering. The pillars, the posts. His hand was pressed to his side to hold back the sharp agony knifing him. Parallel to him, across the aisle on the right, Taylor's big body moved from pillar to pillar, keeping pace with him.

Brent had taken a heavy pistol from one of the guards in the cell fight, as had Taylor. A pitiful armament against General Ursus and his legions but at least something . . .

The keen eye of Dr. Zaius spotted a flashing movement behind one of the pillars on the left. The doctor whirled, his eyes roving. He saw Brent, staggering, lurching to cover.

"Ursus!" Zaius shouted in alarm. "Behind the pillar!"

The General had rearmed himself with the rifle of one of his climbing troops. His reflexes were lightning-like. Spinning, his eyes finding what Dr. Zaius had seen, he fired. The blast of the gun rose like thunder in the arched cathedral.

Brent went down, clattering to the floor with a muted blurt of pain. As he tried to rise, Ursus fired again. Brent lay there in the darkened aisle, waves of nausea and agony closing over him. He moaned. A whimper. The Bomb, unnoticed in the excitement, had separated into two closely adjacent sections. In falling down, it had divided. Part of the steel casing began to glow strangely. But Ursus and several of his apes had come down off the high altar, circling, moving in on Brent.

Across the aisle, his lungs bursting, Taylor sprang toward the dais, on which stood Dr. Zaius, the Bomb and the dangling apes behind him.

"Zaius!" Taylor yelled.

Zaius saw him, recognized him. The orangutan face split in a shock of surprise. He recoiled as if Taylor were a leper.

"You!" he gasped.

"It's Doomsday, Zaius." Taylor spoke bitterly from the depths of the front row of pews. "The end of the world. Can't you understand? For God's sake, help me . . ."

"Stay away from me," Zaius said, backing away, looking for the armed support behind him.

"You damned animal!" Taylor thundered.

He started to bring up his gun, coming on to the high altar, reaching up to the *prie-dieu*. Zaius scuttled forward. "Don't touch that," he warned. Frantically, he signaled the guards.

"Help me," Taylor pleaded. "Help me." His eyes, in the dim light, shone like stars. Zaius shook his head.

"You asked me to help you. Man is evil—capable of nothing but destruction."

Worn, spent, bleeding, Taylor sagged along the edge of the dais.

"You bloody bastard," he panted helplessly.

"Evil," Dr. Zaius repeated, his voice rising. "And the destroyer himself must be destroyed!"

Oblivious of the dialogue on the dais, General Ursus had closed in on Brent lying in the darkened aisle. Brent stirred painfully, bringing his pistol up. Ursus bounded forward in a prodigious leap, his powerful legs landing him directly across Brent. He seized Brent's gun hand, and bit with his great jaws into Brent's forearm. The gun clattered to the floor. Ursus scooped it up, beaming. He motioned to the accompanying soldiers to kill Brent. His eyes swept to the platform where Dr. Zaius stood pointing a gun at the battered Taylor who had lifted himself to the high altar. Taylor was now only twenty feet from the Bomb. General Ursus knotted his fists.

"Fire!" he commanded Dr. Zaius. "Fire!"

But Dr. Zaius was indecisive. There was a look in Taylor's eyes that he did not understand. That was beyond his range of science. Men do not look at you that way when they are not in deadly earnest.

Taylor limped to the *prie-dieu*. He reached it.

Ursus bounded forward, cleared the platform, raced toward Dr. Zaius. As the baffled apes hovering over the prone Brent hesitated, Brent's dying gasp called out, echoing in the hollow reaches of the cathedral. "*For God's sake, it's the Doomsday Bomb—the end of the world!*"

Snarling, General Ursus snatched the weapon from the hands of Dr. Zaius. He aimed the gun at Taylor and fired. Taylor's back was to him. An unmissable target. Ursus did not miss. The blast of automatic gunfire stitched across Taylor's massive back, hammering him down to the floor before the *prie-dieu*. Amazingly, Taylor staggered erect, lurched forward and toppled over the *prie-dieu*, like a tired orator clutching his lectern. General Ursus growled in his chest. Dr. Zaius was rigid with growing dread. The great shining Bomb, with its passengers of great apes still in position on it like so many children, glowed more strongly than ever. A strange aura of *something* pervaded the stage.

The great stain of blood on Taylor's back spread into a river of red. Through blood-curtained eyes, Taylor saw the cathedral spin all about him, whirling, coruscating, like a kaleidoscope. His senses fused and he died, slamming down over the bejeweled panel board.

He never saw the End.

The dead weight of his big body pressed down on the ruby button on the panel. The one that had never been touched before.

General Ursus stared at the Bomb. The glow evanesced over a period of seconds. General Ursus' mouth opened and his fangs showed in a tremendous, terrified scream.

Dr. Zaius had no time to think about anything else. Not in this world or any other.

The ape militia scattered about the cathedral, three hundred in all, stupid, belligerent, unthinking, did not even think of running. Not that running would have helped.

The great cathedral was visible for only one second more.

Taylor's dead body blackened to a silhouette, while above and behind him the Bomb whitened to an incandescence more blinding than the sun which Taylor would never see again.

And then the universal fire began . . .

. . . and all that was left was melting and burning. And small, blackened wisps.

An electronic crackling sputtered in Outer Space.

15   ARMAGEDDON

Listen, if you have the ears to hear.

The Wind is speaking again.

" . . . *the Universe, at present, contains billions upon billions of spiral galaxies. In one of them, one-third from the edge, is a medium-sized star . . .*"

Only a small, blackened wisp. If you have the eyes to see it. Or the heart to care.

"*. . . and one of its satellites, a green and insignificant planet . . .*"

Blank, white, glaring.

"*. . . is now dead.*"

Silence.

There is nothing more. There is nothing left.

It is as it was in the Beginning.

Wasteland.